PURE REVENGE

PURE REVENGE

The Secrets that Lie Within

Robin Munro

Cover Design: Rachel Garay

Cover Photograph: Shutterstock.com

Photograph: Cheryl MacLennan

Editing: Adrianne Norwood

ISBN-13: 9780692199794

*"I've always been a fighter. If you tell me
I can't, I'll die trying to prove you wrong."*

R. A. SALVATORE

Acknowledgements

Wow, what a journey! To write Pure Deception was a feat in itself and now I bring you Pure Revenge. Where I found the time is unclear, but who has always stood by me is very clear and unwavering. I would like to thank many of you that I knew and did not know that supported me whether purchasing my book, providing your place for a book signing, or just messaging me with encouraging words. Many of you know who you are, but I will start with my family. Thanks to my family and my son Justin for his tireless patience, devotion, and encouragement to write this second book. My father, god rests his soul, always somehow in my ear pushing me to never give up, and all of his family that continued to push me along the way.

Thanks to all of the radio personalities and bloggers that reached out to me to promote my first book Pure Deception on their shows. Sheryl Jones, Queen of Hearts, Kevin & K'Ceva Barnes of My Better Half, Derey Alston, The Alston Collaborative, Gary Wade with G-Wade Radio Show, Kim Jackson, Jaye Delai Show, Dee Dee Walker Show, and the infamous Charlie Brown. Thank you Jimmie for opening up your salon and Brenda for telling everyone you knew to read my book. Debbie and Lars at Scandinavian Comfort in Indianapolis, thanks for my Indy book signing and Judy my BFF, Donna (RIP), and David for your help with organizing that for me. Thanks to all of my friends in Indianapolis and other cities, such as Dallas, Ft. Worth, Atlanta, and Memphis that supported me and my Facebook friends that purchased my book and provided their reviews on Amazon. Of course, Rachel for my book covers and Rob for always being by my side. You both know I value your friendship and you have been steadfast having my back. Again, thank you Theresa. You remind me to keep it moving. Marie you have always been one of my biggest cheerleaders and Dr. Denise. Dr. Myint I'm still standing. Thank you Dominque even though you were going through your own crisis, you were always there to support. Stay strong Tina. Art Jackson, thank you for giving me the freelance gig to write for Smooth Jazz Magazine. Your assignments allowed me to continue to perfect my craft. Kesha and Regina even though sometimes I would tune you out, I was always listening. Your wisdom has been my guide. Thank you Ms. Norwood the best editor ever. To all of you with your well wishes, cards, flowers, and encouraging words in Messenger a huge thank you. I have paid attention to everyone that has crossed my path whether positive or negative and took the opportunity to take it all in and learn from it. One thing I have learned through this journey is hitting rock bottom can make you humble and stronger in ways you could never imagine. Learn from your journey. And finally, take all the craziness you have encountered in your life, put it in a box, and label it "Thank You and Goodbye."

Prelude

What is Pure Revenge? It is the highest level anyone can accomplish when they set out to make an individual pay the ultimate price for how they feel they were wronged. That is what Dr. Richard Casey pursued during the course of an ugly divorce when his wife, Amanda Casey, discovered he was having inappropriate relationships with patients, amongst other indiscretions. Instead of facing the truth, he hid behind his lies and denied doing anything wrong. With that being said, he sought out revenge on her. He was like a thief attempting to accomplish the biggest heist, but unfortunately, he got caught. He was a sore loser and took it to a level that was unimaginable. In the end, he fell on his own sword in the book Pure Deception, but still refused to be defeated. So now, he is seeking revenge again in a different way.

On the other side of the coin was Amanda. She was fighting at every turn, angle, and punch brought to her and she was relentless trying to circumvent the revenge that was originally initiated towards her. She had to use revenge to protect herself, not as a dagger like Dick to get back at anyone. It was her tactic as a survival mechanism in this battlefield of a divorce to maneuver through the land mines she had to dodge and grenades thrown her way. Be very careful when seeking revenge. Beware of the old adage "An eye for an eye and a tooth for a tooth." It can cause mental fixation to the point you are incapacitated to make sound decisions. Seeking revenge is tactical and planned. It has to be executed to the upmost precision or it will turn on you and you are the one getting burned. Be careful with revenge. It is not for all to seek and all to handle coming out smelling like a rose in the end.

New Beginnings

"The first step towards getting somewhere is to decide you're not going to stay where you are."

Jᴏʜɴ Pɪᴇʀᴘᴏɴᴛ "J.P." Mᴏʀɢᴀɴ

Cold and dark like a dungeon as he sat in his bedroom cave looking out of his window as the rain pummeled down sideways; his mind working overtime reflecting on the chaos that put him in this wheelchair confining him like bars on a cell. Currently leasing a one story home a far cry from the beautifully appointed home he once had with Amanda. Sitting afflicted surrounded by four pewter walls that were now the vault that encased his existence. Frustration, angst, and defeat the current canvas of Dr. Richard Casey's face, although his ever present cocky demeanor lay intact. All of his calculated theatrics and his false presentation selling the courtroom as the victim. He took pride at his underhanded approach to cement the fate of Amanda Casey his goal to leave her penniless after the divorce, but karma ran the course of his game and gave him exactly what he deserved. Adjusting to life in a wheelchair was a new beginning for Dick, his first step to overcome being outmaneuvered at his own game. The beautiful blonde wielding shots in the courtroom perfectly placed a silver bullet that found its way to shattering Dick's L2 vertebra and required a Neurosurgeon to place rods and screws to stabilize his spine. After spending a month in an inpatient rehabilitation facility, and still traveling down the road to a long recovery, all he could focus on was how convenient it was for Amanda not to be in the courtroom that day and how it should have been her and not him taking that stray bullet. While in the rehab facility in the middle of the night, his screams could often be heard echoing off the sterile walls, like an injured soldier wounded during combat, obviously having a bad dream.

He shouted, "It should have been that bitch that got that bullet not me!"

Constantly battling his mental struggle or more like a mental breakdown; making his current situation one that was going to be very challenging to conquer. But remember, winning at all cost was his mantra and the war he unleashed on Amanda did not provide the results he anticipated. He was going to do everything he could to beat this initial setback and make a comeback; walking again and taking back his earnings. With his initial goal underway, his next plan of action was not only to get to the bottom of how all the money Lenny had stashed away had disappeared, but also how he could get it back. Now he felt the despair and strife Amanda felt when he tried to leave her and Ryan high and dry. Dick was determined to fight his physical handicap while mentally trying to fight the demons inside that were speaking to him and telling him to take revenge. Struggling with his demonic thoughts; it was going to be difficult to seek revenge, because he had apparently found a spiritual being he never worshiped before, God. As many people do when they hit rock bottom, Dick started praying. With each progressive move towards healing, he became more devoted.

Paralyzed from the waist down with no feeling or connection, he sat in his wheelchair listening to the storm brewing outside and reading his Bible as he waited on his Home Health nurse to arrive and begin his therapy session. He caressed the smooth, crisp pages while he read Deuteronomy 4:29, "But if from there you seek the Lord your God, you will find him if you seek him with all your heart and with all your soul." As the words touch his conscious, his newly found faith leaped to fight his handicap. Dick swore he could feel the brush of the spirit as a tingling sensation ran throughout his entire body. Rubbing his Bible like it was a genie in a bottle waiting to correct his circumstance. He then turned to a page he book marked in Romans 12:19 and read aloud barely audible "Never take your own revenge, beloved, but leave room for the wrath of God, for it is written, "VENGEANCE IS MINE, I WILL REPAY," says the Lord.

The doorbell rang and Dick placed his Bible on his lap and wheeled himself through the dark hallway to let his therapist in.

"Good morning, Dr. Casey. How are you feeling today?" his therapist Jacob asked him in an upbeat fashion.

"Hey man, I'm doing well despite this temporary setback and ready to put in the work. I am definitely going to get through this," Dick said confidently closing his Bible.

Jacob smiled with enthusiasm. He was excited he had a patient that was not only a doctor, but one ready to tackle this uphill battle by holding on to his faith in God, and willing and upbeat to defeat his current challenge with God's favor. Jacob wanted nothing more but to see Dr. Casey walk someday. Dr. Casey felt the same way and with his confident new found faith of arrogance, he knew he would.

*   *   *

Wearing smiles from ear to ear as if they had just walked on the red carpet at a film premiere, Amanda and Landon arrived back in Dallas. Holding hands while making their way through the terminal, Amanda reminiscing on a wonderful getaway from the events that had transpired while they were on their retreat. Beaming more so than on her wedding day with Dick; she did it. She beat him at his own game, Checkmate! As the luggage was moving at its usual snail's pace, Landon reached over and kissed Amanda on her forehead her mind still floating in the clouds about her victory. This gesture somehow grounded her back in reality and reminded her of her mother. With how quickly everything had transpired, she neglected to call her mom, Carole, and fill her in on everything.

"Hey babe, I need to call my mom; I am sure she is worried about me," Amanda told Landon.

"Take your time; that's important plus I need to call the club anyway and let them know I am back and get my clients scheduled for the work week," he said not wanting to let go of her hand.

Amanda knew her mom was probably pacing the floor putting a hole in the linoleum, but she had to keep her away from the last court proceeding because it was finally taking a toll on her health, as well as her mental state. She didn't want to risk her mother's diabetes and blood pressure getting increasingly out of control than it already was since her mother's friend, Dot, called to tell her she wasn't compliant with her medications. And based on the episode that occurred in that courtroom, she might have had a stroke or a heart attack. Thank God she was spared from being exposed to that.

"Hey Mom," Amanda said very upbeat.

"Amanda honey, I have been worried sick about you. I tried calling you and you weren't answering, and not hearing from you made me think the worst when I saw that crazy woman shooting on TV. I was so afraid something very bad had happened to you. You sound good," Carole said with some relief.

"Mom, I am fine and that's why I am calling you. Give me some time and I will tell you all about it. I just wanted to let you know Ryan and I are more than okay and your next trip down here will be a vacation. I am putting you up at the Four Points Spa and Resort for a week of pampering and relaxation."

"Honey, I am all for relaxing, but you can't afford that right now," she said with a bit of curiosity like her statement might be a question.

"Mom, I can. I will fill you in later. I just wanted you to know that I'm fine and I will touch base with you later," Amanda tried to sound confident and convincing.

"Okay and take care honey and one more thing…"

Carole had to have the last word and needed to get her point across.

"Yes Mom," she said starting to get irritated with the extended exchange keeping her from Landon.

"Don't take this wrong, but I saw what happen to that asshole Dick, and I am glad he got everything that was coming to him. That joker thought he had the system beat lying about his financial situation and running around chasing skirts like he was a teenager. He ought to be ashamed of himself, but as long as you two were married; he thought his shit didn't stink. I bet it stinks in that diaper he has to wear sitting in that wheelchair. I couldn't have asked for a more appropriate punishment for him. The way he treated you and Ryan, his ass is exactly where he needs to be," said Carole jubilantly.

"Mom you are going to make your blood pressure go through the roof talking about him."

Amanda's mother had a way with words, and when it came to Dick, she could go on a rampage. What she said, however, was quite comical and Amanda couldn't help but chuckle.

"Now that we are talking about how you feel, are you taking your medications on time and following the doctor's orders?" Amanda said in a non-confrontational way.

Carole could go zero to one hundred when you questioned her about taking her meds. But as usual she ignored Amanda and said, "And finally Amanda, give my grandson a kiss for me okay?"

"I will mom. I will talk to you later, and please take care of yourself. Take your medicine mom!" Amanda said exasperated. If she only knew what else had taken place, she would have had her on the phone the rest of the day.

Amanda then dialed Stevie to schedule a meeting to discuss the latest events and what should happen next.

"Hey Stevie, I'm back," said Amanda like Jack Nicholson did in the movie The Shining.

"Amanda, you are really funny, got jokes, and you sound great. It must have been a good vacay, Huh!" Stevie said a little jealous.

"No jokes, just relaxed. You ready to meet," she said full of new found energy.

"Absolutely, just tell me where baby girl," he said excited to see her.

"Let's go back to our spot," she said just as excited.

"Club Admiral?" said Stevie with a chuckle.

"Yes, that's our spot."

"Okay, me and Neko will meet you there".

"Great! Let's meet tomorrow around six in the evening."

"See you then," Stevie said fantasizing about Amanda and how she would look relaxed and tan instead of anxious and on a mission like she had during their previous encounters.

Stevie and Neko were like brothers to one another, cut from the same cloth with regard to life's tragedies and had a lifelong history together. The traditional two parents in a home was a luxury that was not bestowed to either one of them. Stevie was raised by his mother he worshiped and adored. He eventually lost his mother to the hands of his father, and lost him to the penitentiary, which did not matter to Stevie because his father was lost to begin with. Filled with hate and resentment for his father for murdering his mother, he vowed to never see another woman hurt the way his mother was. His grandmother took over the role of mom and raised him. He idolized her for coming to his rescue and loved her dearly until tragically when he was fifteen, she was at the wrong place at the wrong time. While leaving the grocery store after buying food to prepare for him, she was brutally murdered by stray gunfire from rival gangs. He was left alone and forced to raise himself. His only way of survival was the last thing he wanted to do and that was turning to the gangs. He wanted to right a wrong and reorganized the gang he was associated with to not have innocent people victimized by what they were trying to accomplish. He was good-looking, hardworking, and well liked so his reorganization worked. Neko, on the other hand, was a jock in high school. He was proficient in baseball, football, and basketball. He was actually being scouted by many universities and on his way to receiving a full ride college scholarship for football to one of the universities in Michigan. He was 6 ft. 2 inches, half Latino and half African American and could have been a male model. He had won the Golden Ticket until he blew out his knee his senior year and was to never play again. Depression set in and he too lost family, his mother to cancer his junior year of high school and he never knew his father. He knew he was destined to have money and fame, but his path was no longer clear after his injury. His only alternative he knew to at least get paid was to turn to the local gang, The Latin Crew, and that's how he met Stevie. Stevie took Neko under his wing and they have been family ever since.

Stevie's assessment of Amanda's situation was a very easy pill to swallow and he had no qualms about helping her. To Stevie, Amanda was beautiful inside and out. She was no nonsense, smart, funny and turned heads as she walked by. This was a woman he would do anything for forever.

After Amanda hung up with Stevie, she walked toward Landon, who was still on his phone. She was smiling until she saw an unfamiliar scowl on Landon's face. Once he hung up abruptly, she asked him, "Is everything alright?"

"Yes. Just my high maintenance clients upset I took time off for myself. They are just a bit demanding," he said thinking of the quick excuse to deflect Amanda's question.

Typical Amanda shrugged it off and then the light bulb went off in her head that maybe she needed to pay closer attention to Landon. High maintenance client equates to a high maintenance female client that was not only unhappy he was gone for so long, but unhappy not knowing where he had been, or who he had been with. She had not paid attention to the signs before with Dick and the toll it took on her was one she could not endure again. She saddled up to his side and tucked herself under his arm to make him think she didn't notice the little lie he just told her, however, she made note of it and wouldn't forget it. Finally, their bags arrived on the carousel and they headed for his home.

The entire drive back she sat in silence pondering how wonderful a time they had together on their vacation. Landon was great and she enjoyed being with him. Her life experiences, however, had Amanda wondering if Landon was too good to be true.

Walking on Sunshine

"I'm walking on sunshine (Wow)
I'm walking on sunshine (Wow)
I'm walking on sunshine (Wow)
And don't it feel good"

KATRINA & THE WAVES

Spring arrived in Dallas in full fashion. Magnolia trees, Crepe Myrtles, and Bluebonnets were in bloom from the fields alongside the freeway finding any place they could to showcase their glory. And with that, Amanda's allergies celebrated the beginning of spring weather, but she was not going to let that get her down today. She was in a much better place than the spring before reflecting on the dreadful divorce, her gross negligence of failing to see the lies, betrayal, and deceit of the ex-husband, Dick Casey. She was looking forward to better days as she drove to Club Admiral to meet Stevie and Neko. Accidently hitting the tune button on the radio, it landed on a station that played 80's music and the song playing was, "Walking on Sunshine." A smile spread across her face as the song was a perfect theme music. Cranking the radio up not only for the upbeat tempo, but to enhance the mood she was in and how timely the song was for creating the vibe. With a bouncing upbeat attitude, she parked her car and immediately pulled in next to Stevie and Neko. This time they weren't in a Mercedes but in a black shiny Porsche Panamera with chrome wheels.

She got out of her car and screamed, "Why are you two driving my dream car?"

"Your dream car Amanda?" said Stevie with a raised eyebrow.

"Yes! This was the car I was planning on purchasing with the Texas vanity plate reading 'HisLoss,'" Amanda said meaning that in so many ways.

"Damn Ma, I mean Amanda, my bad," said Neko.

Shaking her head she thought, *Same old Neko, still can't call me Amanda on a good day*.

"I am so not into fast fancy cars, but with my new found freedom from the hell I had endured I felt I should treat myself and this car is the ticket and I deserve it," she said proudly.

"That you do Ms. Amanda, so I will get with my guy and we will get the title and all the paperwork in order so this car is yours," Stevie said happy to oblige.

"But one more thing Amanda, your plate shouldn't say 'HisLoss.' That plate baby should say, 'I1MYWAY," Stevie said longing for Amanda, but trying his hardest not to show it.

"And that I did," Amanda said shaking her hair as it flowed in the wind.

Amanda was beaming like a young teenager at her sweet sixteen surprise party that got the car she was dreaming of, but never thought she would get. "Let's get inside and get caught up before I forget why we are here and how much do I owe you for the car?" Amanda chuckled.

Neko smirked and then Stevie announced, "Don't worry about the car. The dealer owed me one so just take it as my gift to you."

Totally caught off guard and not knowing what to say she stuttered, "Thank you, Stevie."

Even though it was 6 pm the place had an after work business crowd. You know, the men that dreaded going home to their Stepford wives, businessmen closing late deals to a lap dance, and your usual suspects hoping to have more than a dance after the dancer got off of her shift.

They walked to the back corner of the club. The same darkly lit spot they had their meeting to orchestrate a plan for Amanda to get what was rightfully hers. It also was the secret location she placed the infamous plain white cocktail napkin that had Dick's name inscribed on it and landed him in a place he deserved, but she did not intend to select. The cocktail waitress came by to take their drink order and they waited until she returned with their drinks before they discussed why they were there.

"Amanda, as I told you on the phone, we took care of our boys, twenty-five each for them and they are back in Detroit as we speak," Stevie explained taking a sip of his beer.

"So what is in the coffer?" she said after tasting her wine.

"The what?" Neko said slightly confused.

Amanda chuckled, "Neko what is left in the pot, the bag," and before she could finish, Neko whispered

"I gotcha now, or in the trunk." He said finally understanding what she meant.

"Is that where it is?" she said slightly giddy.

"Yeah, all eight with five zeros behind it. You never told me how much to give my guys, so I made an executive decision," Stevie confirmed.

"That's fine but how are we going to make this transaction?" she said.

"Easy. We just going to put it in your car Ma, I mean Amanda," Neko stuttered and then laughed almost spitting out his drink of Hennessy.

"I can't go to a bank and make a deposit like that!"

She took a big gulp of her drink with the weight of receiving such an amount and how to deposit it now sitting on her shoulders. She couldn't even remember the max amount you could deposit in cash without tripping some reporting requirement at the bank. A flash of heat ran through her body as the pressure ruined any and all relaxation she felt just a few moments a go.

"Amanda, we need to get you a safe for now and you gradually put money in your account over time, or like your ex did, just put different amounts in several banks. You got plenty of them here that's for damn sure," Stevie said.

"That sounds like a feasible option. I owe you a lot so what is the price tag for your services," Amanda stated in a businesslike fashion.

"Amanda, that's up to you," Stevie explained as he took Amanda's hand into his.

Amanda began to blush and another flash of heat ran through her from a totally different source, which only caused her to blush even more. She didn't understand her reaction nor Stevie's body language and his caressing of her hand. Trying to not make too much of his affection, she did the same thing like the last time they were here, she took a plain white napkin and with the number in her head, she wrote two, zero, zero, zero, zero, and one more zero.

"Is that okay with you?" she said as she passed the napkin across the small table. Stevie reached for the napkin and their fingers touch again. This time they locked eyes making the exchange pause in time.

Slightly delayed, Stevie pulled the napkin close and took a glance and then confirmed with his partner before saying, "That's fair I get one and Neko gets one, an even split."

Neko nodded his head after glancing at the napkin one more time and taking a sip of his drink. He added,

"Amanda if anything else pops off, you know we got you."

"This may sound premature, but I'm starting to get an unsettling feeling with my guy Landon," she said with uncertainty.

Stevie interjected, "What's he doing to make you feel this way?"

"With everything I have gone through with Dick, I pay attention to everything now. It may not be anything, but if any of my suspicions continue to fester, I will definitely call you. Thanks guys. Let's enjoy our drinks and finish our transfer outside," She said looking a little embarrassed over her confession she hadn't meant to share, but somehow felt comfortable sharing that information.

While smoke filled the ceiling of the strip club, Stevie looked up into the darkness making a mental note of what she said about Landon. Sipping his drink, he smiled thinking about the man she really needed was him. Before they went to the car to make the transfer, Amanda was enjoying the atmosphere and Neko and Stevie's company once more. She twirled her wine looking in her glass as if it were going to speak to her providing her answers; pondering what was going on with Landon and his peculiar curious behavior. Her confession to the boys made her intuition about Landon a bit more real and left a bad taste in her mouth, which could have also been from drinking wine at a strip club.

By the time they finished their drinks, Amanda was pretty sure Neko was well on his way to spending half his earnings in promises to a curvy blonde. Stevie had to untangle the two in order to get him up and out of the club. Amanda noticed him apologize for his rudeness with an undetermined amount of green. He was rather polite and smooth. As if reading her thoughts, he looked at her and used the same palm to guide her out of the club with a gentle touch at the small of her back. Amanda couldn't have been happier for the cool night air that brushed against her face and filled her lungs. With the cover of nightfall, Stevie and Neko unloaded one trunk and filled the other. They departed with nods and the whole way home Amanda felt like she was driving with illegal items in her possession. She contemplated what to do with the bags and finally decided on hiding them under her bed until she could find a safe to store the money. She'd make her first small deposit in the morning.

Too Good to be True?

"From my experience, honey, if he seems too good to be true-he probably is."

CANDACE BUSHNELL

Crashing waves of the ocean, the intensity of the sun, and beads of water falling off of Landon's chest as he slowly walked out of the water towards her at the beach cabana. He straddled the beach lounger and then her iPhone Alarm started to wail. Dreaming about the wonderful getaway she and Landon had, she dialed his number as she made her way to the kitchen to make coffee, he answered.

"Hey beautiful, you beat me to the punch. I was just about to call you to see what you had planned for today. You got our coffee already made?" he said smiling.

God his accent gave her goosebumps and so in tune with her routine.

"I was just about to make my usual Dark Roast Coffee, and I was planning to go to work today," she said with slight hesitation.

"Amanda you sound like you don't want to go in and I wouldn't blame you now that you got your situation with Dr. Casey in check," Landon chuckled.

"Please don't mention the devils name. I want to get my day started right and on a positive note," Amanda said.

"Come on baby lighten up, but I understand. Have you thought about just taking some more time off? You have gone through more than most" he said sincerely.

"Yes and no, but I don't want to cloud my head thinking about that today. My alarm woke me up from a wonderful dream I had about our vacay," she said longing to be in his arms at that very moment.

"I've been replaying that vacation in my mind as well. It was magical. You want to grab dinner later tonight?" he said seductively.

"Let me call you a little later. I need to find out what's on Ryan's schedule with regard to school and what's going to happen at work today."

"Okay babe, I will wait for your call." Landon said very excited.

Immediately after Landon hung up with Amanda, his phone rang. Without looking to see who the contact was, he answered.

"Hey babe, did you forget to tell me something?" he said.

The voice on the other line was silent. His gut clenched since he got a phone call like this when he was in the airport waiting on the luggage with Amanda and quickly made up a little white lie about his high maintenance clients. He listened a bit and then ventured another, "Hello?"

Heavy breathing was the only thing he heard and before he decided to hang up suddenly a voice yelled, "No! The question is did you forget something? You thought you could get rid of me; throw me away as if I were trash!" The angry female voice spat.

With a scowl on his face, rage and fear shot through him and he hurled the phone hitting the wall, which cracked the screen.

"Damn it!" he screamed.

That voice was the woman he fell in love with, Nikki. She was the previous relationship he totally erased from his mind and thought he had escaped unscathed. During the course of the relationship, he discovered that she had some mental issues and erratic behavior. He did his best to be supportive and understanding, but the relationship got to such a toxic level that he could not deal with it anymore. Landon, in his mind, did everything he could to end the relationship without any ill will or confrontation; she just wasn't having it. One unusually warm morning, he woke up to what sounded like a car skidding off. Running outside to investigate the ruckus, he found his breakfast baking on his car. Approximately two dozen eggs smashed strategically on his BMW. It was taxing trying to get that crap off and the guys at the detail shop got a good laugh. After that event, she resorted to stealing plates off of his car, which he didn't always notice. This resulted in being pulled over by the police for not having plates on more than one occasion. Each time he would have to explain the embarrassing situation to the officer about her egging his car and how his plates had disappeared; he reported the tags stolen and got new ones more times than he cared to admit. When stealing the tags wasn't enough, that crazy bitch would think of something else to torture him with. Like the time, she camped outside his place and slit all of his tires. The final straw was setting his car on fire. If she could have, she would have set it ablaze with Landon in it. He couldn't prove it was her, but it didn't take a rocket scientist for him to know it was. The insurance company with their multitude of questions and investigation, you would have thought he had set his own car on fire. And of course, that is what they thought had occurred. They took him through the ringer on that one. She even threatened a woman at the gym that was a client, because she thought she was his love interest. Her craziness almost destroyed his career along with his car. Not even her psychiatrist was of any benefit. With HIPPA Laws providers of care for patients cannot divulge anything about the person they are treating without written permission. She had Landon on all documents to share information about her care. The psychiatrist, Dr. Connelly advised against it, but Nikki would not have it any other way. Dr. Connelly would apologize for the events on her patient's behalf, but wouldn't provide any solutions other than for Landon to start coming to see her as well. Landon was infuriated at the lack of help for himself and for his ex, especially after numerous conversations with the psychiatrist about concerns for Nikki's well-being. Landon was at a loss of what to do next. Crazy, insane love can make individuals do unconceivable things and for his own safety, he left. He moved, bought a different car that wasn't like what he would usually drive, and changed up his schedule just to throw her off is track. Landon felt like a convict wrongly convicted trying to escape to get his freedom again. His life had finally settled down and he thought it was over, but it looked like it was far from it. Now she was stalking him. I guess that's what happens when you let your guard down. A vengeful ex with a snake's venom he never saw coming. Landon picked up his phone and sat down hard. Placing his phone between his palms and resting his head on his praying hands, he whispered, "Dear God I have found someone I want to be with, please get Nikki out of my life for good." He shook his hands with fervor with his eyes raised to the sky, as if he were willing his prayer to reach up faster.

* * *

Amanda got Ryan off to school and headed to the office for her weekly healthcare marketing meeting at CFY Healthcare Corporation. All the while pondering if everything was okay with her and Landon. It felt right, but intuition was kicking in and she didn't know how to process it. Her gut told her to put on her armor to protect her heart. Her heart spoke to her whispering let love back into your life. As she parked her Porsche Panamera at the other tower parking garage so no one would see her, she inconveniently ran into one of her counterparts, Kristina. Kristina is a young, tall, extremely beautiful go getter in the company that is like a little sister to her, but can't keep a secret if you paid her millions. Feeling flushed and nowhere to run or hide, she put her big girl panties on to face whatever was about to transpire.

"Amanda, is that you?" said Kristina smiling with curiosity.

"No it's not, who wants to know?" Amanda said with laughter.

"Honey did you get back with the good doctor? Kristina said dying to know.

"No honey, I just got back at the good doctor?" Amanda bantered back.

"Well if you are not back with that psycho ex-husband doctor, then who is he?" Kristina said not able to wait for the response and said, "And does he have a friend?"

"Kristina you are one crazy girl. No, I have a friend and he is out of town so he wanted me to keep his car while he is out for a while," Amanda said thinking she dodged a bullet.

"Amanda you are so damn secretive; I didn't know you had a friend like that."

"Kristina, let's keep it like that. Pretend you don't know I have a friend, and let's get this meeting over with before you start an inquisition in front of individuals that should not be concerned," she said in a very serious tone.

"Okay Amanda, let's go into this meeting. But remember, I see you," Kristina said grabbing Amanda's arm like two school girls walking to class.

About midday, Amanda decided she was going to listen to her heart for now, and dialed Landon's number to meet. Landon answered quickly, "Hello babe. Are we on for tonight?"

"Yes. Sorry I haven't called you sooner just trying to tie up some loose ends at work since we were on vacation." When in reality she was undecided thinking too much about what would happen if she continued with the relationship.

"Hey you sound like you have something on your mind. I can whip up something fabulous for us if you would like and we can hang out here," he said in an overly accommodating tone.

Ugh! She thought if she took Landon up on that offer, she would never leave. She finally answered him, "No, I would like for us to go and grab something if that's okay. Where do you want to go?" she said, longing for his touch and to see his infectious smile.

"There is a new Thai restaurant that just opened in close proximity to both of us," he offered.

"That sounds great just text me when and where and I will be there."

"Is 7:00 a good time and I will text you the address?" Landon said tentatively and sounding a bit anxious.

"Yes, I will see you then," she said curious to see his face and wanting more than dinner.

After work and an exhausting day of deflecting endless questions from Kristina, Amanda raced home to make sure Ryan's sitter and he were doing his homework before she felt comfortable to leave to meet Landon. As a mother, Amanda always felt a bit neglectful leaving Ryan again after just returning from vacation and since he didn't have a normal father son relationship with Dick anymore. Of course, Ryan and Dick didn't have a healthy relationship before Dick's misfortune and they certainly don't now. His inability to do anything athletic with Ryan doesn't allow the two of them to do much, but Dick didn't do that much with him when he was physically capable anyway. After finalizing the divorce, Ryan was sympathetic to his situation, but was appalled, disgusted, and embarrassed by Dick's behavior who was to be an upstanding physician and a so called father. Once reality had sunken in, he was forced to face the gravity of Dick's actions during the course of the divorce. So much so, that Ryan refused to participate in the required visitation schedule per the divorce decree. The most interaction Dick could muster up were self-serving text messages to Ryan.

"Hope you are well son. I really miss you and want you to know that an important key to success is self-confidence. The key to self-confidence is preparation. I love you! Love Dad." Dick wrote. Why in the world he sent that text and what it meant, only his warped mind knows?

One of his more fabricated text was, "I am sorry that your mother has brain-washed you into thinking I did some awful things. I have not. If she were a better wife, none of us would be in this precarious situation. I love you! Dad."

Same old Dick, writing that text to prove in his mind that he was a good father and to convince himself he never abandoned his son making himself feel better. One thing is for sure, Ryan is not confused now and that is why I think he decided to distance himself from Dick. He didn't even call him Dad anymore. He calls him Dick. To make matters worse, his friends don't even give him a title such as Ryan's dad, Mr. Casey, or Dr. Casey. They just call him Dick as well. She felt like such a loser mother not being able to protect Ryan from the hurt he was feeling not having a real father. Taking him to therapy and counseling over this crap proved challenging, but Ryan's response at the last session shocked the therapist and Amanda.

He said to the two of them, "I am so glad this is our last session. This was a total waste of my time and yours. You want to know why? It's because telling you all what is going on with me and how I feel is not going to change anything."

That was difficult for her to swallow and she needed to continue to make Ryan a priority. Juggling the relationship with Landon and trying her best to make sure Ryan's needs were being fulfilled was a challenge to say the least. Plus, Ryan was getting older and enjoyed his space more than he enjoyed his mother hovering around like a "helicopter mom." Hiring male sitters was Amanda's way of providing male role models that were likely a lot better than Dick.

She needed to stop stressing so she could manage them both. Fortunately, dinner with Landon and hopefully dessert after would be all the relaxing she needed.

It's Not Over; It's Just
Getting Started

Oh, my friend, it's not what they take away
from you that counts.
It's what you do with what you have left.

— HUMBERT HUMPHREY

A demon in his mind kept telling him that Amanda was somehow responsible for his money being confiscated and Lenny being bloodied and battered. That demon had taken root and the feeling of truth consumed him even though he had no proof yet. Reading Corinthians 10:6-13, conflicted with the mental combat of taking matters into his own hands or maintaining his faith attempting to live a Christian life was challenging at best. He tried to find some clarity reading Corinthians 10:6-13 interpreting the reading, "It ain't over until it's over." One thing was for certain, his physical therapy session with Jacob went well and he felt like any day now he was going to have some feeling in his toes and legs again. Determined to walk again and Amanda, well she is going to get whatever God deemed should come to her one way or another whether it is by his hands or His hands. The phone rang to Dick's surprise.

"Hey man, how are you?" said the husky voice of Lenny.

"I'm keeping positive man," he said trying not to display his displeasure with Lenny's half ass attempt to get the job done he hired him to complete.

"Lenny do you think Amanda has my money?" Dick said still perplexed.

"Man, I don't know but you can't underestimate your ex. If she did, she was in cahoots with some guys Vernon knew from up north that are really no joke, The Latin Crew. Was it a coincidence, who knows? If she was behind this, it's a mystery how she could be connected with The Latin Crew," Lenny said sounding deflated and lucky to be alive himself.

"Well if it's her, she might think she has won this round, but I have some ideas of my own," Dick said vehemently.

"Vernon is lying low because he has pissed off some people in those same circles; he is in fear of some sort of retaliation. I don't know if we can get him on board again, so what you want me to do doc?" said Lenny.

"Man watch your back, I hate the fact they found out what we were doing and almost killed you and now Vernon's wellbeing is in jeopardy," Dick said in an apologetic, uncharacteristic tone. But then in an instant Dick's ugly head surfaced to say, "Lenny we have been friends for a long time, but find my money! I was willing to divide our assets and be rid of Amanda and make sure Ryan had what he needed and hoped he and I could be, well, be in a good place, but it was your idea to take it all. So get my money Lenny," Dick spoke to his best friend now like he was the enemy.

"Man, I understand and I will do everything I can to take back what is rightfully yours," he said with a stutter.

"Also, I paid you and Vernon a descent amount of money during the divorce to get that done," Dick reminded Lenny.

"I will get it taken care of," Lenny said with a tone of remorse.

"Just get back with me and what you need to get this done." Dick said.

Longtime childhood friends should be near and dear to your heart, but when it came to money, Dick had loyalty to no one. He felt satisfied putting Lenny on notice that it was not over by a long shot, he was just getting started.

With the unsettling feeling of fleeting loyalty from his friend Lenny, he was refusing to get comfortable in that wheelchair with a plush leather seat; he saw the finish line and he knew he would be walking across it, not rolling across it. Pushing one hand into his temples and the other hand aggressively rubbing his brow, he began to wonder where Taylor was. How could she have left him? Even Amanda stood by him in difficult times, why couldn't Taylor? And so what if she was a patient; he wanted her and she wanted him. Lots of guys have a side piece while portraying to their colleagues they were model citizens and great husbands to their wives and amazing fathers to their children. It didn't matter who you were or what you did, doctor, lawyer, fleet driver, chef, athlete and the list was long. That's the game that's played, but he never thought he'd be so sloppy as for Amanda to find out, or was he so cocky to think she wasn't smart enough to figure it out. That was water under the bridge; he knew he was going to walk and soon, and then get Taylor back. He couldn't stop thinking about the times spent sneaking in the house he and Amanda shared while she was away taking Ryan to visit family or on a girl trip in the Caribbean or away on a ski trip. Then he had to be quite discreet and get a hotel room close to the hospital. He was really convincing how busy he was at the hospital and Amanda bought that shit like she was buying a Chanel Bag from Neiman Marcus. Spending time with Taylor at the Best Western Elite Hotel and slipping the Hotel Manager, Brandon, some cash on the side to keep his extra-curricular activities quiet, was all he had to do. Taylor didn't require the luxury of a Ritz Hotel or any other five star hotel like Amanda. It was so refreshing to date again and feel wanted and needed, and the thrill of spending time with Taylor and not getting caught was an adrenaline rush. Amanda could have cared less as long as she could wine, dine, and shop. And of course dote on Ryan with all of his activities he participated in such as soccer, football, basketball and tennis. He really wanted to be there for his activities; he just couldn't get there. Plus Amanda was Superwoman and wore that title well. Dick liked that because all he had to do was go to work, screw Taylor and a few others he had on the side, and visit the gentlemen's club from time to time. Life was good and he had it all, well until the fiasco in the courtroom. Rest assured he was going to get everything back including Taylor.

*"Trust is like a mirror, you can fix it if
it's broken, but you can still see the
crack in that mother fucker's reflection."*

LADY GAGA

Comfort and contentment should have wrapped its arms around Amanda and provided her with the confidence she needed to continue moving forward. In a sense it did. The warrior that lied dormant in her came out in a blazing force and showed Dr. Casey take caution when dealing with a woman scorned. With her dream car and plenty of cash, she threw caution to the wind and ignored Stevie's advice of lying low. Instead, she bought a cute updated one-story bungalow beautifully landscaped with a saltwater pool in University Park, and Ryan had plenty of space to hang out with his friends. No wrought iron heavy door when you enter this home like her previous one; that door serving as a vault to hide secrets. The new home had a beautiful wooden door easy to open that was welcoming and a start of a new chapter in her life. She still applied for a mortgage, which was only approved with the large all cash down payment offered. Dick purposely not paying for the household bills during the course of the divorce to prove to the judge he was broke put her credit score in a number she didn't even know existed. She also had Landon and the ink had finally dried on the divorce decree. Hesitant to meet any new neighbors not wanting to entertain new actors into the soap opera of a divorce: she was pleasantly surprised to meet a divorcee like herself, but not quite like her. Her new neighbor's name was Elizabeth and she came from a very well established family that owned half of Wisconsin. She was ten years younger than Amanda and had two boys around Ryan's age. They slowly interacted and the boys definitely did not have a problem hanging out, so it worked. Amanda finally felt like she was in a place where she and Ryan belonged. She should have felt calm and at ease in her new surroundings and living a new life. Lately, however, uneasy feelings of uncertainty had taken over as if she were at war again without seeing the enemy.

Before she could allow those thoughts to consume her mind, the phone rang and it was her best friend and Ryan's Godmother, Jessica.

Before the phone could even hit her ear she heard Jessica talking. "Amanda I know you have a lot going on, but I think I need your help." Sounding as if she was out of breath from running a marathon and all she does is play tennis like she is Serena in a Grand Slam Final.

"You are making me nervous Jess, what's up?" she said afraid to ask.

"I am too embarrassed to even tell you because you might scream at me and I am so not in the mood for that," Jessica said tearfully.

"Tell me what?" Amanda asked frantically.

"We are losing our house!" she said sounding like she was at her wits end and still sounding breathless, possibly sobbing.

"What do you mean you are losing your house?" Amanda screamed.

"Amanda I trust you with my life but David has... well, he has hidden things from me amongst other things and now we are losing our house!"

"I cannot believe this. Not David, too! Jess, honey, don't worry; I have a little money now and we can keep your house," said Amanda in an angry, but sympathetic voice Jessica had never heard.

"No, Amanda. I don't want you to do that. I really need to speak to you further, but I have to pick the boys up from football practice shortly," Jess let out a frustrated huff.

"Jess calm down. I am giving you an hour to regroup, and then you better tell me what the hell is going on. I have never heard you sound this desperate or upset," Amanda said like she was fed up.

"Okay. Okay. I will." Jess hung up without another word.

After that unexpected news from Jessica, Amanda's mind started to spin out of control like she was reliving her chaotic experience with Dr. Richard Casey. The underhandedness, undermining, calculated behavior she experienced would never be something she'd wish to bestow upon her friend. But yet the frantic urgency in Jessica's voice brought back all of those horrific memories she was trying to bury. With all of her previous drama, did she contaminate her best friend's relationship with her husband? She couldn't let it go and watching the clock like a hawk, within an hour she called Jessica back.

"Hey Jess, you totally caught me off guard and in some way I feel somehow responsible for what you are going through. Please be a little bit more explicit," she said in a firm you better tell me everything voice.

And with that Jessica started bawling out of control worse than her initial call. To hear her cries, reminded Amanda of the initial pain she felt at Dick's betrayal. Her heart sank to the floor with a thud. She couldn't even formulate words; her tears and cries mirrored pure heartache.

"Jess I am so sorry. I wasn't trying to upset you, but after my disaster of a marriage, I can help you. What the hell is going on?" she said now finally wanting an answer.

Jessica, Amanda's best friend since grade school and over forty years of friendship, was confronted with her own marital crisis tsunami. How could this happen? She was the epitome of a happy healthy family life and marriage. She tried off and on to be a shoulder for Amanda to cry on, and hated Dick with every ounce of anger she could summon. How could a boulder fall off a cliff and land on her head? This was too hard for her to fathom. She had it all, like Amanda thought she had it all and then some. These two women treasured their families and their friendship. Amanda felt really awful for her.

"Amanda, how could I be so stupid?" Jessica finally half screamed with anger and blurted the sentence quickly between sobs.

"Jess, please start at the beginning. After my debacle of a marriage, please let me guide you through whatever the hell David has been up to. I am an expert with disaster," she said wanting to expound on what I said by telling her I am her FEMA, but this wasn't a time to joke around by any means. "So help me with how you know for a fact that you are losing the house," she said as if she were an attorney trying to get discovery.

"Amanda I found a final notice and multiple notices that David hid. He hid these notices in his car glove box. When he was out of town last week, on business, so he said, I thought I would surprise him and have it cleaned. It was so disgusting; I really wasn't paying attention to the papers and bills. As I was going through the inside of his car, I found notices and my intuition told me to open the glove box and that's when I discovered he had been hiding not paying our mortgage for months!" Jessica started immediately crying again. I couldn't tell her not to cry because I felt her pain. I knew how painful betrayal was so I could not fault her for that.

"Jess, you mentioned there were bills as well?"

"Yes. All of the bills he was responsible for were late and our utilities were in jeopardy of being turned off. Now it makes sense when our cable was cut off a few months ago and he told me he paid it and it was a mistake."

As I listened in shock, I carefully asked her, "How was it that you didn't know any of this?"

"Honestly, Amanda I got so caught up on the boy's activities and my work, that I thought my household was on automatic pilot. Anytime I questioned household bills or issues, he had a viable excuse," she said shamefully.

"Jess, you have my support because I lived what you are dealing with, but just a little bit differently," Amanda shared with reassurance. "What I am going to need you to do is find out how much is owed and I can get it caught up and you decide if you want to keep the house or sell it. Also, find out what utilities may be in jeopardy so we can get that taken care of as well," said Amanda in a commanding voice.

"That's not all," Jess said with a pause.

"Really Jess there is more?" questioning what additional mud she was going to sling.

"There are notices from the IRS that not only do we owe them, but there are some years we never filed, and of course there's the other family I think he has," Jessica said very casually.

And with that, Amanda felt as if she was free falling and a hard landing would never wake her up. She was beyond shock and confusion. This was pure deception all over again and happening to another strong, smart female who was blinded by her picture perfect male. Hesitant to ask additional questions to her last outburst, she just couldn't help herself and she said, "What other f…f… family?"

There was total silence. She thought the phone was dead or maybe Jess hung-up.

Finally, JESSICA sighed, "And now Amanda, I understand very well all the pain you had endured with that asshole Dick."

"*Definition of a victim: a person to whom life happens.*"

— PETER McWILLIAMS

Dick was nervous as he searched for his lost love. He kept wiping his palms as they perspired. Then he spotted her, finally after a long, unbearable search. Her beauty mesmerized him as always with her flowing auburn reddish hair and the butterflies danced in his stomach. How she could affect him so after all this time and all that he'd been through? She was sitting at a corner café with her long legs crossed drinking coffee and flipping through a magazine. She looked so heavenly and peaceful that he didn't want to disturb her. Dick had searched too long not to though. The car stopped. He wasn't driving, but paid no attention to the driver. Instead, he opened the door and carefully placed both feet on the sidewalk. Looking at his reflection of the cars exterior, he confirmed he was one handsome devil, which gave him the confidence he needed to walk right up to his long, lost treasure.

"Hello, my love," Dick said as charmingly as he could, unable to think of a better pickup line. She looked up and recognition made her eye widen ever so slightly. "May I join you?"

Taylor was eyeing him up and down and her jaw dropped slightly, but not enough for her to lose her picturesque image. She finally managed a soft, "Yes."

"We have so much to catch up on and I have missed you enormously." Dick reached out and took her hand.

Time morphed and he saw visions of them walking hand in hand, smiling, living richly, and happily ever after. Then, he felt a strong tingling sensation. Panic struck him and he woke up startled. Imagination can play tricks on the mind when something is desired so badly. It didn't feel like he was imagining anything. The dream felt so real, like a premonition. Then the tingling started again and he recalled what woke him from his glorious dream. Tingling! He couldn't register the sensation at first, but he could feel it in his toes. Dick's eye shot straight to the ceiling as he thanked God for this confirmation. He was on his righteous path. He was meant to find Taylor and be happy again and when he did, he would be walking. She was going to apologize to him and make amends. They were going to be together again. Dick may have been a victim of circumstance, but the tingling he felt reaffirmed this was only temporary. Anticipation and anxiousness rolled through his body as he pushed himself up from the bed. Dick could not wait to share the change of events with his therapist, Jacob. Before the therapy session, he needed to find out if Lenny had made any progress on locating the money. This was also foreseen in his dream and he had to make it so. Lenny would have a new assignment as well, finding Taylor as he now knew she was key to his mobile future. Dick reached for his phone and dialed.

"Lenny, what's up?" Dick said cheerfully.

"It's going man. I've got some guys trying to track down who and where the money may be," Lenny said without being asked. He knew Dick would only be calling for one thing.

"I need you to do me one more favor," Dick said excitedly.

"What is it man? I know I owe you," Lenny said knowing he owed him more than a favor.

"Can you help me track down Taylor?"

"Yeah doc, you say the word and I will get it in motion," Lenny said trying to redeem himself.

"Lenny I am saying the words; find Taylor," he said a tad bit pissed off.

"Got it; it's done," Lenny replied knowing he better get this right.

"Give me updates on what you find out and I will be waiting. All I have is time," Dick said slightly peeved; the joys of the dream fading as the minutes passed after his waking.

"Hey, Doc I told you I got this," Lenny said as if it was already done.

After Dick hung up from Lenny, his thoughts were, *if Lenny didn't get this right he was definitely going to be sorry.*

Dick put down the phone and got ready for his appointment with Jacob. While his battle with his anger was a daily struggle, Dick recited verses to himself while he dressed.

Lenny's thoughts were whom does he think he is talking to that way? He better be glad he was in that damn wheelchair, or he would get Vernon to have one of his boys to straighten his ass out. Lenny was the one that came up with the plans to make Amanda destitute and Dick was all for it. He may have underestimated Amanda, but he better stop the dictator shit. Lenny didn't take kindly to individuals that were ungrateful whether they were a friend or family. He had plenty of resources that he had not shared with him, so he better stop being so damn demanding. Vernon and Lenny helped orchestrate Amanda's proposed downfall; Dick made them his handlers. If she was behind this, she was fortunate enough to stay a step ahead of them or her ass would have been left disabled or in a body bag. But that shit was short lived, and Lenny will make sure he gets Docs money back so he can get what he earned. Vernon was a little gun shy hoping the gang didn't take him out. The heat was on his ass making that fire a bad predicament. Now that Amanda may have infiltrated what he thought was his safe haven, he had to find a way to shut it down and get that money back or Vernon may be in a lonely dark place in a box or in ashes way too soon.

Lenny paced around his makeshift office as he thought. The faster his mind worked with plans the faster he paced. By the time he felt like he had a good plan forward – or so he hoped.

Victor

"He who knows when he can fight and when he cannot, will be victorious."

— Sun Tzu

The sun dancing radiantly on her face with its heat beating down through the sunroof as DJ Khaled's song "All I do is Win" played on the radio. The words in the song were so fitting describing what she had accomplished. It became her anthem song. As she was cruising down the freeway, music blaring in her Black Porsche was reverberating. Had she really won? A sense of adulation and victory running through her body the thoughts of inflicting pain on Dick in many ways; taking the money he thought he could steal and his evil attempt to destroy her, but it maimed him. Keeping her plan under wraps dodging her attorney to avoid accidently divulging the plan worked. She needed to call Mr. Cartwright's office though because she really had forgotten what she signed off on finally. In addition, she wanted to be sure he was okay and she was more than curious to hear his version of what happened. That man thrived off of hearing the latest antics of Dick and found humor when it came to his indiscretions with his sex addiction. She could imagine his animated commentary about the occurrence in the courtroom.

"Law office. This is Holly."

"Good afternoon Holly, this is Amanda Casey. Is Buck in?"

"Oh Ms. Casey you were on my list to call. Buck wanted you to schedule to come in. I'm sure you heard what happened in the court room," she said wanting to go into more detail.

"I heard alright," Amanda said wanting to burst out with laughter.

"He has documents for you. Are you available any time today?"

"I am actually. Can I swing by at 2:00?" she asked.

"I have you down and we will see you then," Holly replied.

Running errands prior to meeting with Buck, the thoughts of how and what she was going to say, if anything, about what really happened clouded her brain and she wondered if any of it would haunt her. Before pulling up to Buck's office, her mind was racing and reminiscing about all of the times she and her mom, Carole, spent in that office with their blood, sweat, and tears. It was like more tears than anything meeting in that office before court and after court trying to combat the antics of that asshole Dick Casey. Feeling concerned about her mother's health since their last conversation; she decided to call her.

"Hi mom. How are you feeling?" Amanda said upbeat.

"Oh I am so glad to hear your voice honey. How are you and my wonderful grandson doing?" Carole said.

"Mom we are fine. I was just checking up on you to make sure you are taking those wonderful pills the doctor had prescribed," she said jokingly in hopes not to piss Carole off.

"Honey, I am fine. I am taking my meds and it's a glorious day. I am well and able. I go on walks with my girlfriends. That's more than I can say for that sorry ass ex-husband of yours, because all the walking he has comes on wheels baby" Carole said in a scathing voice.

Did I hear my mom correctly? Did she say "on wheels baby"? Trying to pretend that she did not hear that last comment she said, "Well mom you do sound good, but I want you to come down and enjoy The Four Points Resort soon. Please tell me you will take me up on that," Amanda said wanting her mom to come so she can really see what she was up to.

"Honey, let me look at my schedule and I will let you know," she said.

"Okay mom you better make a decision quickly, or I am going to make it for you and book your ticket," Amanda said firmly.

"Alright Amanda I promise I will let you know."

"Love you mom!"

" I love you and my grandson honey. I will talk to you soon," Carole said trying to get Amanda off of her back.

As she approached Buck Cartwright's office, out of nowhere he pulled up beside her. He never parked in the front of his office. Damn! She had some explaining to do with the expensive car she was driving.

Screaming like he did at Dick in the courtroom, "Amanda, what in the hell are you driving and better yet, that plate "I1MYWAY"?" he said sounding confused.

"I love you too Buck and I'm glad you noticed my vanity plate," she said very animated.

"Well young lady, you got some explaining to do," he said with a chuckle.

"It's very self-explanatory; I won my way," she said uncharacteristically cocky.

He escorted her into his office and Holly asked if she wanted something to drink. She responded, "If you have some shots, I will take that."

"Shots!" Buck yelled.

She looked at Amanda with confusion so Amanda tried to make it very simple and said, "Holly, water is fine."

"I will bring it into Buck's office," said Holly not knowing how to respond.

While they were settling in Bucks office he yelled again, "Linda don't come into my office yet; look outside at that black shiny ass car Amanda parked in our lot with that damn Texas vanity plate!" Returning his attention to his guest, he lowered his voice a notch. "Amanda that asshole you divorced did not give you enough money to squat in, and as I recall you were on food stamps during the course of the divorce. So how in the hell did you get that car?" he said wide-eyed.

"Buck I know, but I did not have faith in the legal process so I took matters into my own hands," Amanda said with her head slightly down.

"Please tell me you haven't resorted to participating in some shit where I cannot represent you. I practice Family Law not Criminal Law Amanda," he said in his brazen voice.

"No," she said and before she could explain, Linda walked in the office grinning ear to ear.

"Okay, I see both of you looking at me like I robbed a bank, and yes I did," Amanda said jokingly.

Buck and Linda looked at her stunned.

"I am kidding. Oh my God! Yes I robbed a bank. Dick's secret bank," she said screaming out of frustration.

"Amanda I'm a busy man and don't have time for this shit. So what are you trying to say and say it fast because I'm losing my patience?" said about to go on one of his normal tirades.

"I was fortunate to meet some individuals that had resources we were not privy to and devised a plan to help me find what Dick was doing and where he was hiding the money he lied about in court," she said proudly.

"How did you do that?" Buck said about to start his belly laugh.

"I can't give away how I pulled off the heist, but I got tired of the legal back and forth charade and took back what he tried to steal. I would have liked him six feet under, but my heist had nothing to do with the courtroom activities. Dick is cruising around in his wheeled chariot, but I made sure it wasn't made of gold," she said unapologetically.

"I couldn't even find the damn money Amanda. I am not going to ask any more questions, but I am impressed I must say," he said like a proud papa.

"I know you were limited trying to go by the book and abide by the law. I decided to go another direction and fight to get not only what I needed to provide for myself and Ryan, but my retainer and finder's fee for being instrumental in getting Dick's solo practice up and running," she said emphatically.

"So how much did the good doctor stash away?" he said.

"The exact amount he said he didn't have $900,000," Amanda said happily.

"That son-of-a-bitch kept moving the money; I couldn't keep up with it. You sure you don't want to share how you found it and better yet, how you got it?" Buck prodded.

Linda finally chimed in after picking her mouth up from the floor and said, "Does he know what you have done?"

"I am not sure but with help from his devious goons; I am sure he's trying to put the pieces to the puzzle together, and when he does, I must be prepared for what he may have in store for me. I am glad I'm here to put you on notice that if something happens to me; it was him," he said slightly concerned.

"We are not going to think like that right now Amanda, but I thank you for filling me in. You know I don't like to be blindsided," he said sincerely.

"Blindsided should be my middle name with all that he took me through, and all he had to do was split what we built together," she said angrily.

Buck and Linda shook their heads in agreement with Amanda's assessment as Buck provided Amanda with the provisions of the divorce decree. She hugged Linda, waved at Buck and left the office speeding away in the black shiny car to address Jessica's issues. Any concerns Amanda had were going to have to be put on pause. The friend that was there for her during her hard times needed her, so there was no way she was going to let her down.

As she left Buck's office, her mind settled in to simmer over Jessica and her situation. She found it quite unbelievable that now her best friend was going through the same kind of spectacle. Another man lying and cheating and stupid enough to think he could get away with it. We do so much for our men and this is how they repay us. With a glance at the speedometer, Amanda realized her speed had increased a little too much like her anger was at the moment. She let her foot off the gas and took some deep breaths. Jess wasn't ready for drastic measures – yet, but there had to be something to help. Tossing around the idea of a vacay with Jessica after her divorce, Amanda was going to make it happen.

Jess definitely needed the getaway like the way "T" and Amanda did in Miami without the thrill-seeking encounter of a Stevie or Neko.

Amanda loved those guys. They were her life line. Amanda had the keen sense that Jess didn't want to leave her boys with all of the unsettling shenanigans of David and knew she would need reinforcement so she decided to call her sister Debra. Staying a step ahead of Jessica when it came to her boys posed a challenge but Amanda was prepared to get them situated so she did not have a reason to turn her down for a quick girl's getaway. While entertaining the idea of a girls' getaway, she called "T". It had been awhile since she got back in town and wanted to catch her up on Landon and better yet, Dick's misfortune, or should it be said his stroke of bad luck.

"Hey "T" how are you doing and did you hear what happened to our beloved Dick Casey?" Amanda said laughing.

"Amanda it is so good to hear from you and most of all, to hear you laugh again, those tears of yours could cause a river to overflow immediately. To answer your question, yes I saw the news and I was floored. I couldn't have written a better script. From the sound of your voice, you must be on a natural high," Tamara said sounding excited to reconnect.

"I am on a natural high right now, but when I think everything is on cruise control; commotion and craziness seems to continue to follow me," Amanda said little apprehensive.

"Now what? Please don't tell me that paralyzed lame ass Dick continues to be a thorn in your side," Tamara said in disgust.

"He hasn't yet anyway. We only communicate through our attorney's which is fine with me. And poor Ryan doesn't really want to be bothered with him. Dick has been extremely quiet which scares the shit out of me. It wouldn't surprise me if he had his flunkies conjure up an alternative plan for me, because that bastard doesn't give up that easily," she said.

"Well always watch your back."

"Tamara, don't worry about me. I am smart enough now to know he may eventually seek his revenge. It is my girlfriend, Jessica, Ryan's godmother that I am worried sick about now," she confessed.

"Oh no! What is going with her?"

She is in some deep marital discord and the professional I have become with this situation; I will support her and make sure she gets through it. It's just like the Pitbull mentality you had standing by my side with that psycho Dick. I am trying to take her on a girl get-away similar to our entertaining one in Miami. "T" that got me through the beginning of my saga and I thank you for it," she said with much appreciation.

"Oh my god Amanda, that was a crazy good time and I am so glad we met Stevie and Neko or I don't know what would have happened to you," Tamara stated elatedly at the memory.

"I know what would have happened. I would have been destitute the way Dick planned. I am thinking about taking her away and that's part of the reason I had to call you. So, what's been going on with you?" she said inquisitively.

"Well Bryan and I are getting along better since he forced me to remove myself from your drama," she said with remorse.

"I figured as much, but I understood and you have always been there for me. There was no way I could be mad that he wanted his wife back," said Amanda sincerely understanding that she had to preserve her marriage before it ended up like hers.

"Well, I have a little secret to share with you. I have a special friend and we were in Mexico when the chaos occurred in the courtroom," she said with giddiness in her voice.

"What? Amanda I want to hear all about it. This is so not like you. I want to know everything," Tamara said smiling through the phone.

"I will get you all caught up later," she said not wanting to tip her hand that there may be danger in paradise.

"Okay. I cannot wait to hear all about it," said Tamara with excitement.

"I want to take Jessica to a great place to relax and play tennis," said Amanda.

"Well, I read that Cove Island in The Caribbean has a great place for relaxing, unwinding, and yes they have great tennis pros," Tamara said as if she wanted to go.

"Tamara I will definitely check it out and if you want to hop on board, feel free to join us," she said trying to convince her.

"Let me see what Bryan has scheduled for me," Tamara said sort of prematurely disappointed.

"I am glad we got to briefly catch up and I will be in touch," Amanda said with hopes she may want to tag along.

Thinking of another girls' trip made her smile. Being with Tamara in Miami was such a blast and she wanted Jessica to experience the same with her being the shield to block out what's in store for her upon her return. Plus you never knew whom you'd meet or what crazy ideas might come to light.

As soon as she hung up from Tamara, she saw a call coming in from Stevie. He must be able to read minds.

"It's a great day at I1MYWAY. How can I help you?" she answered with laughter.

"Amanda it seems like every time I call you, you have something funny to say. You make me laugh pretty lady," he said beaming.

"Well this is an unexpected call, somebody is thinking about me. Are you trying to save me again from the big bad wolves?" she said smiling.

"If need be, absolutely. I was calling to check on you. Is that okay with you, Ms. Amanda?" he stated wanting to see her for any reason.

"Of course it's okay. How are you and Neko doing? Is everything okay?"

"Everything is fine. Neko is still Neko. I just had you on my mind," Stevie slipped.

He had a lot on his mind but didn't know how to express it. Amanda, who isn't short on words, was speechless. The silence was earie. He couldn't believe he said it out loud and she couldn't believe what she heard. The silence only lasted a few seconds, but it made Stevie a little unsettled, so he mustered up the courage to speak again.

"You still having some questions about your man Landon?" Stevie said making an attempt to take the conversation in another direction.

A little caught off guard she said, "Somewhat, but I am hanging in there with him for now."

"Well, if he gives you any trouble or he is not treating you the way you know you should be, all you have to do is call me," he said with a very serious tone.

"Stevie, I know I can count on you," she said feeling his heartfelt concern.

As her body became warm, she changed the tone of the conversation yet again by throwing out, "I might need your services for a friend of mine, Jessica."

"What's her situation?" he said excited that he may be able to see her again by helping her friend.

"Another crazy husband with deceitful ways and possibly living a double life. I don't have all of the specifics, but I am taking her away from the madness like Tamara did for me, which is reminiscent on how Tamara and I met you and Neko."

"Well let me know when you need us. I am always there for you Amanda," hoping she would say she needed him right now.

Man was Tamara a distraction and a blast when they were in Miami. Amanda was on the verge of a nervous breakdown, and she did not want her friend Jessica to remotely experience what she did. Amanda was pulling all the punches planning this trip. Her other distraction was Landon, but lately she felt he seemed to be the one distracted. They had a great dinner last week and she showed great restraint not to have a nightcap at his place. He wanted her to go home with him, and she was having Landon withdrawals, but felt like he had something on his mind he just couldn't shake. What had his mind preoccupied she couldn't pinpoint, but at some point, she was going to find out. With the divorce chapter finally closed, she had two new missions aside from her normal duties: 1. Plan the best trip ever for Jessica and, hopefully, Tamara; 2. Play investigator and find out what was up with Landon and the gut feeling she just couldn't shake.

You've been down before
You've been hurt before
You got up before
You'll be good to go, good to go

— Fifth Harmony

Jessica's sister Debra followed Amanda's orders to take care of her nephews so Jessica couldn't back out of the much needed break in Cove Island. Amanda called her so excited about what she had in store for them.

"Hey Jess, you ready to have some rest, relaxation, spa treatments and some great tennis?" she said pumped up like a contestant competing on a game show.

"Amanda I really would like to go, but I don't want to waste your money by not having any fun," she said sounding disappointed.

"Well my friend, you do not have a choice. I have made all the arrangements and the boys are already being taking care of by your sister. I hope you are not offended, but the tickets are confirmed and I have made arrangements to get you packed, rackets and all," she said in a commanding voice.

"Which sister is watching the boys?" Jess said sounding very upset.

"Debra is watching the boys Jess. Is that okay?" Amanda said very confused considering she didn't think she had issue with her sisters.

"That's fine. Well it looks like I am going away on a trip Amanda," Jess sighed sort of relieved.

"Yes you are and we are leaving tomorrow," Amanda said as if her mission was accomplished, but very confused on the comment on who was watching her boys. Immediately after hanging up from Jessica, her cellphone rang and saw it was Landon.

"Hey babe, what's up?" she said totally neglecting to inform him of the last minute plan to get away with Jessica.

"I was just checking on you. You busy?" he said sounding so sweet.

"Well, I am in the process of packing for a last minute trip."

"A trip? Where are you going?" he said slightly confused with a tinge of insult.

"I don't know if I told you or not, but Jess is going through what I did with Dick, so I am taking her away for a long weekend to Cove Island," she said hoping he wouldn't be upset.

There was a long pause and then he softly said, "Okay. Where is Cove Island?"

"It is in the Bahamas and we are going to connect, enjoy the spa and play tennis, which she will kick my ass at," she said laughing, but Landon did not find any humor in it.

"Well Babe be safe and have a good time," he said sounding sad.

"Landon, as soon as I get back from my time with Jessica I will call you immediately. I will miss you, but I need to get my girl in a right place."

"I understand. Please be careful and I can't wait until you return," he said like he would never see her again.

"Love you," she said.

"Love you more," Landon said.

Oh shit! Why did she say that, but it was too late. Crap! Her brow furrowed as she thought about what just happened and continued to pack. Frustrated with not knowing what all to take with her and why she couldn't take back words, she left her bedroom in search of a glass of wine.

*   *   *

This adventure almost didn't happen. Jessica, God love her, with everything going on she couldn't find her passport. She had never been out of the country and Amanda asked her to apply for one awhile back with thoughts that her divorce would be over so quickly they would be celebrating and basking in the sunset somewhere internationally. It shouldn't have been a surprise there would be some kind of glitch. Jessica could be ditzy at times; multi-tasking to the point she couldn't find things or forgot. She reminded Amanda so much of her mother. God rest her soul. Jessica called all in a panic, but once Amanda guided her to trace her steps and recount her possible placement of the passport, she found it in a box of pictures she had pulled out. She said as she was packing for the trip with her passport in her hand, she found a box of pictures of her boys. She started reminiscing looking at baby pics to present pics, and pictures of David and the boys. Somehow she inadvertently placed the passport in the box with the pictures.

After that fiasco, she confirmed to herself that she needed to get away. As she drove to the airport, Jess was full of nerves with one hand on the wheel and the other digging around double-checking she had everything. Assured she had everything, her anxiety was still at a high level. When she entered the airport and passed successfully through security, she took an audible exhale. The time for worries and frets was over. After a short connecting flight from Indiana to Charlotte Airport, she would meet up with Amanda, who would be waiting for her after her connecting flight from Dallas. She prayed both would arrive safely into the Charlotte Airport and from there they were going to the Bahamas. A black town car was waiting at the airport to take them to the Cove Island Resort, like the very important people she was looking forward to being for the very short trip. Amanda arrived in Charlotte first and found the gate where Jessica was to arrive. Her flight was on time and if she weren't one of the first passengers off of the plane, it would have told her she missed the flight because she had them flying first class for their roundtrip. Poof and like magic she was the fourth or fifth person off of the flight. A sigh of relief came over her and tears flowed because she was so glad to see her. Running towards each other like sisters reunited for the first time after being separated, they gave each other a very long hug.

"Jess I am so glad I got you away from that drama, at least for now. I have always loved Debra and she was a godsend taking over so you could make this trip," Amanda said elated.

"I'm not going to lie, I felt guilty leaving the boys with everything going on. I believed I was adding to their confusion," Jess said sadly.

Trying not to minimize her concern, but offering reassurance that it was a good idea Amanda pointed out, "The boys are probably glad you are gone, because Debra is going to let them run all over her."

Jessica laughed and said, "You are probably right."

"Relax Jess. You need this trust me," said Amanda knowing she was going to be in for a fight if David had been as deceitful as she described when she received that dreadful call from her.

"We better get going. I don't want us to miss our flight," Amanda said sternly.

And with that they rushed to the gate to commence the Cove Island adventure.

* * *

Intoxicated by the atmosphere and the beverages they were partaking, Cove Island was the therapy they both needed. She needed it as a temporary sedative to her current situation, and Amanda needed it to get her mind off of her too good to be true Landon and that awkwardly revealing conversation with Stevie. Tamara was on point about this place and Amanda wished she could have been here. She didn't meet a stranger and would have started a party phenomenon with the amazing DJ that was creating a hedonistic vibe of people dancing, drinking and playing Black Jack beyond the pool bar. As they were lounging in their Cabana and taking in the eye candy, Jess started to open up.

"Amanda I really appreciate your friendship and trying to protect me from that craziness you had gone through. Honestly, I get it. I just don't even know where to begin," Jess said feeling a bit calmer in her delivery as she sipped on a rum punch numbing her body, sun tanning her face.

"Jess, I just want you to share whatever you feel comfortable with, while at the same time, getting this shit off of your chest. Finding out your spouse's deceitful ways can take a toll on the mind and body. Look at me. I am still a hot mess, but I camouflage it like I have it all together. You know from experience that one of the first steps to dealing with this is to let it all out. Once you do that, the rest we can try to solve and work through. Jess we are family. I hate feeling like I am an authority on this, but shit, I am. So start at the beginning," Amanda said with no apology and looking at her good friend like she was ready to listen to it all.

"Like I told you, it was really by accident. Trying to surprise David and ended up surprising myself," As their eyes met and they both simultaneously mustered a laugh.

Amanda didn't mean to laugh when she said that, but she could envision her going above and beyond trying to surprise him, but she was the one that got the surprise. The feeling was like uncovering the biggest spider you've ever seen in your entire life, screaming like you never wanted anyone to hear you scream, and forever being haunted in your dreams by the encounter.

"So have you let on that you know what the hell he is up to?" Amanda said sounding like the detective.

"No. I was so shocked; all I could do was call you. I didn't know what to do," she said still sounding so out of sorts. "And since then I've gone on like normal not knowing how to bring it up or how I wanted to react or afraid to because then it would be more real."

"I get that. I do and we'll ponder that here in a bit. But first, you also mentioned another family he might have. What the hell did you mean by that?" she asked afraid to listen to her response and praying it wasn't true.

"I think Julie has been having an affair with him," she said calmly.

She spewed the sip of drink just put into her mouth out. "Julie! Not your sister Julie," Amanda screamed in disbelief and stood from her chair, like she was ready to go put that girl in her place. A few loungers looked in their direction and made her calm herself back down into her chair. She padded herself with the cocktail napkin while she wiped the shock off her face. Now it made sense when she asked which sister was watching the boys.

Jessica calmly waited to respond until Amanda looked at her again with her less than serene face. "Yes; my conniving ass sister Julie," she said with conviction.

"I thought she was getting married to that landscaping guy. The one she bragged about that was so good at landscaping her," she said in a caddy way and still totally baffled that Julie would do this to Jess.

"Yes that was supposed to happen, but no one in the family knew what happened with that relationship. He seemed to just disappear and no one asked any questions. You know how secretive she can be if shit isn't going her way. She has to always keep up the appearance that her life is so grand," she said as if she didn't care.

"So did you catch them together? It doesn't make any sense," Amanda said still not able to put two and two together.

"Put it this way, they have spent a lot of time together in my presence at the boy's games and other activities I could not attend because of work and I just ignored it. I really don't want to talk about it anymore. I want to enjoy this time away I never get to enjoy Amanda," Jess said.

As they were consuming too much rum punch in the sun, Amanda slurred, "Well rest assured you are in good hands with me this weekend and I really want you to enjoy this time. Sorry for all of the questions. I feel compelled to analyze this situation further to see what I can do to make sure you don't get shafted the way Dick tried to shaft me. I won't allow you to be left high and dry like I temporarily was or better yet go through great lengths to protect yourself," she said confidently.

"Thanks Amanda, you really don't have to go through all the trouble. I really don't think David would do that to me," Jessica said believing her response - mostly.

"It's no trouble, but right is right and wrong is wrong. I thought the same thing Jess, and look what Dick put me through. I want to hope the best for you, but please don't be naïve either. Preparing for the worst could work in your favor," she said trying to protect her.

Jess took a sip of her drink deciding not to introduce all the other things David had done that would make her or Amanda possibly go on the warrior path. She just wanted to enjoy the girl time. She will save that for later.

The music was thumping so hard that you could feel it in your chest, and deafening as they continued to get caught up screaming at one another to hear what the other was saying. It may have been the alcohol that was prohibiting them to effectively communicate.

But with all of that, they continued to enjoy the drinks, vibe, and the sun until the sun was no longer in sight. By the time they made it back to their rooms, they were so tired from the flights and flights of alcoholic beverages that they ordered an array of items from room service. They caught an old movie while eating. At some point, although it became a bit fuzzy after that they put themselves to bed.

They woke up the next morning a little hung over, but had already had a scheduled drill with a pro. Jess was wide awake and ready for tennis. Amanda, on the other hand really wanted to sleep in, but she wanted her girl to enjoy this treat.

"Hey Amanda, are you ready? I can't wait to get out there!" Jessica said with excitement.

"I don't know if I am ready for you to kick my ass, but I am as ready as I can be," she said trying to not show lack of enthusiasm.

They skipped breakfast, which she was glad for because she was pretty sure she would throw it up. The sun stung her eyes as they headed out to the courts, but it reminded her to perk herself up and emulate it. Jess and I actually had an amazing time playing tennis with a pro that made it to the top 16 at the US Open back in her day. She wore me out, but Jessica loved it and wanted more. Once the pro was tipped more than two extra lessons with a look that told her I would kill her if she kept going, the pro told us she had another lesson and shut it down. Thank God.

"Amanda, that was great! Thank you so much for this trip and the tennis was top notch," Jess said with excitement.

"Anything for you, Jess. I am so glad you enjoyed it, but get ready for this evening for the dinner and the nightlife," she said as if she could party like a rock star for a second night in a row.

"I am ready. Bring it Amanda," Jessica said with a new found attitude.

Amanda was thrilled to see her cockiness. That was the Jessica she met when they were younger and in college, then it was dead and buried when she married. Amanda was determined to wear her out and show her there was life after a psycho marriage.

The Secrets that Lie Within

"Confession is always weakness.
The grave soul keeps its own secrets, and
takes its own punishment in silence.

DOROTHY DIX

S itting trapped in captivity as a prisoner in his own body. That was to be his life sentence too agonizing to bear. But that sentence was reversed not by a court of law, but by God. Standing next to his chariot gazing in the mirror at himself, he knew that he was one of God's chosen ones and that his belief would make way to his victory. He was going to defeat his circumstance. As he thought it and saw himself standing there the image brought on an adrenaline rush, like God confirming the truth as the thought ran through his head. The tingling and sensations from hip to toe were exhilarating. Closing his eyes and opening them quickly to confirm that he was not dreaming. Oh those few steps taken, reminded him of Ryan taking his first steps as a toddler. Looking in that mirror like a proud king over his kingdom, his mind was busy at work. "Mirror, mirror on the wall Dr. Casey will have it all," he laughed in a sinister way as he mocked the evil queen's quote from Snow White. He would have it all and his real life evil queen would be torn from her thrown. "Don't settle in just yet, my sweet; I'm getting ready to give you a deathly treat." He enjoyed the smile that spread across the handsome reflection's face.

This was going to require superior acting to keep his recovered abilities under wraps, but he had perfected that skill while married to Amanda. Sliding back into his chair, he picked up his Bible off of his nightstand and wheeled his way towards the door waiting on Jacob to arrive to begin his physical therapy session.

"Hey Doc, sorry I am running a little late, but that smile on your face tells me you really don't mind today. You must be feeling great," Jacob said always with the attitude of the glass isn't half empty but it was always half full.

"Jacob I thought I was always all smiles. I told you I felt tingling in my toes and I am very positive that my recovery is going to smash the record books," Dick said knowing what he had just said was true, which surprised himself because telling the truth had not been a characteristic he possessed. He was so use to lying, that he perfected it. If there was a gold medal in the Olympics for lying; he would have won that hands down.

"I have a specialty group that I can refer you to. They have a great record for patients making tremendous strides with their physical therapy and they are willing to see you," said Jacob.

"I'm all for it. When can I get an appointment?" Dick said trying to sound enthusiastic even though that doctor's appointment is no longer needed.

"I will let them know you are willing to move forward, get all of the necessary paperwork for the insurance to approve it, and we can go from there. Ok?" Jacob confirmed with a nod from Dick.

* * *

Lenny was on his mission to find out who had Dick's money, or their money was more like it. Upon further investigation over a couple days since his call with Dick, Lenny's hard work paid off so to speak. Vernon verified that it was Amanda that had Dick's money. Somehow she hit the lottery finding some members of The Latin Crew to do her dirty work.

"Hey Lenny man I am trying to lay low, but I found out your girl Amanda hooked up with Stevie and Neko of The Latin Crew from some of my boys I know," Vernon said a little nervous.

"Vernon, how could she possibly begin to know how to hook up with them? You are kidding me right?" Lenny said in total disbelief.

"No man, for real. Dick was way too cocky and she went rogue," Vernon said.

"Wow man, I do not know how to break this to him. He is so pissed at us right now that to tell him this will put him over the edge," Lenny exclaimed.

"Well, I am just the messenger. And if I were him, I would leave this shit alone because those dudes are not to be messed with," Vernon continued his nervous tenor.

"Hey, thanks Vernon. I will let him know where we are headed with this and will be in touch with you on what Dick wants us to do. Man, be safe," Lenny said in disbelief.

*"Some people have a difficult time
facing truth and reality. They prefer to
live in a make-believe world, pretending
that certain things aren't happening."*

— Joyce Meyer

After a full-fledged no holds bar getaway with Jessica, it was time for them both to face their own reality. Jessica with deceitful David and Amanda looking over her shoulder not knowing if Dick had found out what she had done while holding suspicions with her new found love Landon in check. They left Cove Island barely in one piece or should it be said Jessica barely left it in one piece. Finding her inner J. Lo, Beyoncé, and Amanda couldn't figure out the other dances she performed on stage at the club, but Jessica had lost her mind. For a second, it looked as if she was going to go into stripper mode. What was going on with her was pinned up for so long, she unveiled the inner beast or the inner pinned up frustration. It was a blast getting her girlfriend she knew forever back for at least one moment, but now they both had to face what they were trying to escape.

Amanda hugged Jess so tightly like a parent does the first day of summer camp. A hug of reassurance and a hug that it was only short lived because they would see one another real soon. As they were both to embark on separate flights back home, Jess to Indiana and Amanda back to Dallas, Amanda whispered in her ear, "You know I am always here for you and if I could fight Dick you know I can fight David,"

"I know. Thank you, Amanda."

One last gigantic hug and they caught their flights to go back to what they were trying to escape from. Tossing and turning trying to buy sleep the whole plane ride back, Amanda's last conscious thought was of how much fun they had and how she was so not twenty anymore.

*   *   *

Arriving back home, Amanda settled in and entertained Ryan with sanitized stories of the trip. Ryan was getting older and knew his mom, so as bright as the kid was rest assured he could decipher or come up with his own interpretation of the vacay with his godmother, Jessica. He knew we had been friends forever, which in teen years meant as far back as he could remember. Ryan loved his godmother and was happy to hear about the trip. Normally when his mom brought up Jessica, it was to tell him a story that was supposed to also teach him a lesson via the adventures the two of them got into when they were young. He usually tuned these stories out, but the one about the one fateful night the two of them weren't forthcoming with their parents with their whereabouts and almost died in a car wreck when they were teenagers was one that gave him chills every time. With that story in mind, he was relieved they both made it to their respective homes in one piece. Amanda had a brief conversation with Landon on the drive home as he was headed out to get a bite to eat. He didn't realize she was back, so he invited her to meet him at one of their favorite spots, Sushi Soko. Feeling quite antsy, Amanda really hoped whatever was going on with him was resolved and they could go back to being in a good place. That place of euphoria and not being able to get enough of one another. Their conversations and how they could agree to disagree and those intellectual stimulating conversations that were so sapio-sexual, that it turned her on even more. However, her heart panged as she recalled her love confession to him before departing for the trip and his return of that confession. There wasn't going to be any rest for the weary as their conversation this evening would surely be strained as they tiptoed around what was happening with him. Her head hurt just thinking about it, but she couldn't go to her usual wine glass to calm her nerves. She had enough alcohol for a while or at least until tomorrow. As she pulled up to Sushi Soko, sweat profusely decided to make an entrance, not a hot flash, but just the pure stress of what she may encounter. Then maybe it was the excitement and anticipation to see him brought this episode upon her. Confused why this was happening, but thank goodness she had some napkins in the glovebox to get herself together. She brushed her hair back nervously, walked into the restaurant and saw those pearly white teeth gleaming as she walked closer towards Landon. He kissed her on her forehead and said, "I really missed you Amanda, and as usual, you look amazing."

I guess I was glowing after all of the sun I had in the Bahamas.

I blushed and calmingly said, "Thank you Landon and it is great to see you too."

As they tried to size one another up and determine where the conversation should go, the lovely server, Summer, came over to break the ice and asked if they were going to order their usual. Landon announced, "Of course, nothing has changed."

Her thoughts were in a flurry with his statement "nothing has changed" as if to imply that things were changing that were out of his control, but he was going to make sure that did not happen.

"So Amanda how was the trip and how is your friend Jessica doing?" Landon said inquisitively.

"It was great to see Jessica again and to get her away from her current situation. Of course, she excelled in our private tennis clinic we took with a pro, and the resort and its vibe was what we both needed?" she said and then realized she should not have exposed that she needed to get away as well. And of course, that was Landon's opportunity to question why the must needed getaway.

"So Amanda you needed to get away from me?" Landon said curiously.

"No, not at all Landon. Not at all," she said trying to convince herself and wanting this road they were traveling right now to end.

As their server came over to bring dinner, they both dove into it so neither one of would say the wrong thing to one another. Once the food soothed their souls, they were in a place to continue their dance of a discussion.

After she ate the last Las Vegas Roll she and Landon were both vying for, he was a gentleman and let her chopsticks meet his and let her have it. She then told him, "I did need to get away because, I felt something going on with you that I have never felt before, and it rattled me."

Landon looked down at his empty chopstick and looked up not knowing if the time was right to let Amanda in on his crazy ex, Nikki. The server made her rounds again and Landon asked for Sake. When Landon ordered that, Amanda knew she had to brace herself. Remembering herself grabbing Landon's arm and bracing from the extreme turbulence from the flight as they were on their way to Mexico on vacation, she was prepared for the bumpy ride.

Loyalty

"When people show loyalty to you, you take care of those who are with you. It's how it goes with everything. If you have a small circle of friends, and one of those friends doesn't stay loyal to you, they don't stay your friend for very long.

— JOHN CENA

Lenny confirmed for sure Amanda was behind the disappearance of the money. His communication link was Vernon Mack. It seemed Amanda was lucky to connect with Lenny and Vernon's boys from up North that orchestrated the caper. Dick thanked Lenny and Vernon for their loyalty, but now, they had to deliver and get his money back. It's time for Amanda to experience a valuable lesson when it came to trying to get over on slick Dick. She should have known better. He had to give it to her though; he totally underestimated her ability to fight back. It was a pretty gutsy move on her part. Dick's cell phone started to ring so instead of rolling his wheelchair over to the coffee table to take the call, he stood up straight feeling runway ready. Walking over feeling invincible, he picked up his cell to answer the call.

"Hello", he said as if I had been happy walking for years after a traumatic and devastating situation.

"Hey man it's me Lenny," sounding very cavalier.

"You got any good news for me," said Dick grinning ear to ear withholding inside his good news.

"All I can say is I can show you better than I can tell you. When I get closer to getting the job done trying to track Taylor's whereabouts, I will let you know," Lenny said confidently.

"Okay! You sound like you have this under control so I will just wait for your updates. Thanks for checking in." And with that, Dick hung up the phone and walked back to his wheelchair peacefully thinking about Taylor.

*   *   *

Jessica arrived home with her boys in tow after getting an earful from Debra on how much fun they had. As she walked in the door, she looked at her phone and David had text her that he would be coming home. She was so disgusted with his arrogance of deceit, but she had to keep it together to uncover all of the other skeletons lurking in his closet. She was reveling in the fact that she had Amanda guide her through this maze runner and her loyalty as a friend to make sure she came out on top. As she finished feeding her sons and cleaning up, she decided to go into the basement of the home. She would go down there on occasion to clean up after David and the boys played Xbox or were watching a football or basketball game, and thought nothing of what was really in that basement. Afraid she might discover something to strip her mood, she thought it best to wait until the boys were asleep and she had good Intel on where David really was so she would not be caught. Just to be sure, she decided to call David.

"Hello," David answered. "How was your visit with Amanda in Dallas? Is she doing okay?" he said pretty chipper.

"She is doing as well as can be expected after going through a horrific divorce," she said smirking.

I lied about what was going on with Amanda and what I knew. Since Amanda had the boys taken care of, I had to come up with a good reason why I was going out of town. David knew I wouldn't go anywhere without him or the boys, and he knew I would never leave the country. I had to come up with something plausible so I told him a white lie that Amanda was still going through a rough time and wanted me there with her for support. He heard of Dick's demise, but he knew nothing about Amanda coming up on top financially. And from what I had found out so far about him; it's really none of his business.

"I got your text and wanted to know if you were close to the house so I could warm up some dinner for you," Jessica said trying not to sound pissed off.

"Well, I was but I got a call from one of the managers from the office and there are some plans there I need to review, pick up and bring home. I think I am just going to grab something in a drive thru, go to the office quickly, and then I will be on my way home," David said totally well thought out.

"Alright then, I will finish cleaning up and see you later," she said relieved so she can begin her real clean up job, the basement.

There's A Stranger in My House

"It took a while to figure out
There's no way you can say who you are
You got to be someone else…"

— TAMIA

Landon reached across the table and took Amanda's hands into his and said, "Amanda, I have never hidden anything from you and I truly adore you. You and I have had magic and I want that to continue, but while we were in the airport upon our return from Punta Mita, I received an unwanted phone call. It was from an ex I thought I would never hear from ever again. I was quite shelled shocked to say the least," Landon said still trying to get his thoughts together since the Sake had clouded it for a moment. He continued his explanation for his questionable demeanor as of late. "This individual had many issues that medically could not be addressed," he said sadly.

Amanda looked in Landon's eyes and said, "So what cannot be addressed medically? That just doesn't make sense to me. Medicine is so highly advanced. That appears to be an excuse for an individuals continued behavior, or an excuse that there is no hope for that behavior to ever change."

Landon looked down as if he was too embarrassed to continue and momentarily looking directly at Amanda he told her, "Amanda I fear for your wellbeing. Nikki is very unstable," Landon said painstakingly.

Amanda removed her hands from his, raised them in the air, and said, "So what you are trying to tell me she is crazy, disturbed, and a Lifetime TV drama!" Amanda exclaimed with shock and trying not to bring too much attention to their table.

Landon not wanting to go into too much detail confessed, "If you call setting my car on fire, harassment, threats, and stalking, then the answer to your question is yes."

Her eyes began to well up and Landon attempted to take her hands again to console her, but she wasn't having any part of it. She waved over the server to bring the check, made scathing eye contact with Landon, and said, "After everything I have been through, now this. I thought I knew you. I thought you were sweet, honest, and endearing, but I don't know you at all. You of all people know I don't need any more drama in my life. How foolish I have been all of this time," she said in a sharp tone to the point she wanted to scream.

And with that, she gracefully and slowly removed herself from the table, leaving Landon to wait and pay the bill. She handed the valet her ticket once outside and asked him to hurry, which he did once he noticed the tear that escaped down her cheek. Having a nicer car had its perks since valets kept it up front to show off. In a matter of seconds she was in the driver's seat and sped off in her black shiny car with plates I1MyWAY. It looked as if she hadn't won after all in the relationship department. As she found herself speeding on the freeway, tears streaming down her face, she slowed down to notice a car she had seen earlier, but thought nothing of it. She had a weird gut feeling and wanted to test it. Is it that crazy bitch, Nikki, Landon just told her about, or is she in grave danger because Dick may know what she had done? She floored the accelerator and moved over to the far right lane to quickly exit and so did the silver car that looked like a bullet. Amanda's heart was beating quickly and felt as if it was in her throat. As she took deep breathes to calm her nerves, she thought what better place to feel safe but her local police station. As she was getting closer to the precinct, the driver must have been smart of enough to instinctively know what was happening and completed a U-turn and sped off. Amanda pulled over sobbing hysterically beating herself up for falling for Landon. She knew he was too good to be true and this new information proved it. Maybe she overreacted and wasn't sensitive to what Landon was going through, but if she were honest with herself this was the one drop of worry that broke the dam keeping her together. There was only one person in her life currently that could make everything better for her. She speed dialed her saving grace, Stevie.

"What's up pretty lady?" Stevie answered so happy to see Amanda's call come through.

She could not get her words out for all of her sobbing, but finally mustered up, "Hi Stevie, I just need to talk."

"Amanda I am here for you. What is wrong now?" he said a bit confused, but was hoping it was an issue with Landon.

She proceeded to remind him, "Remember you told me if I had any issues with Landon to call you?"

"Yes!" he said with a net ready to save her.

Amanda continued on with how the evening progressed and the story about the ex, Nikki, and also being followed. Stevie was fuming and ready to catch the next flight out of Miami to be with Amanda.

"Stevie, it's like I had a stranger in my house. I guess I really didn't know Landon at all," she said sounding clearer than when she called initially.

That was all Stevie needed to hear.

"Amanda, baby, I am coming to Dallas. Whoever is following you, I will find out. And has for Landon, forget that chump. I will see you soon," Stevie said in a Marvel hero tone.

"You don't have to come so soon. I was having a moment and that car scared me. Really, I'm, okay," Amanda said with some slight hesitation.

"Anything that gets you that upset warrants seeing you in person. I won't believe you're okay until I see it for myself," Stevie stated. This is what Stevie was waiting for, wanting, dreamed about. His wish is coming true.

"Well, okay. Thank you. I'll see you soon," Amanda let out a breath she'd been holding since she thought she was being followed.

"I'll let you know when I land."

*   *   *

Jessica found her way to the basement fearful of what else may be hidden she didn't want to unveil. She slowly walked down the steps like a bride walking down the aisle knowing she should not marry the groom standing at the alter and thoughts of being a "runaway bride". When she finally made it to the bottom stair, she stood there frozen, "do I say I do, or I don't?" That fear had taken over her body and her senses. She finally walked into the great room area. It seemed pretty safe. Nothing seemed out of place or something that required further investigation. She decided to go towards an area they had stored boxes when they had originally moved into the house, but nothing seemed out of place. As she approached, that was far from the truth. There were boxes moved and slightly opened. She moved towards the closest opened box and started to look and dig inside. Again, she found IRS notices and low and behold a letter from the company that David works for. The letter basically read that his services were no longer needed; they thanked him, and wished him all the success in his future endeavors.

She screamed, "WTF! He doesn't have a job! He gets up every morning, dressed, and goes to work. I just spoke to him and he said that he had to go to the office to pick up some plans!"

As the tears began to build she looked again at the letter, it was dated 2 years ago. He had been out of work for two years, but got up every day to go to work and stated he had to travel for his job. Attempting to put the pieces of this puzzle together, she still couldn't grasp if he did not have a job, where was he going? Why couldn't he be truthful and tell her what was going on? She continued to dig through boxes and his lack of employment confirmed all of the outstanding notices found. Some of the letters and collection notices were never opened. He just stuffed them in boxes in hopes that he could bury them and they would go away forever. Who was this imposter Jessica was living with? Not able to continue on she decided to call Amanda. She would be able to help her navigate through this walk of shame.

"Hi Jess. Are you relaxed from our vacay?" Amanda said excited to hear from Jessica since their getaway.

"So sorry to be the bearer of bad news Amanda, but I have come back to more than just secrets, but the upmost betrayal," she said sadly and trying to control her emotions.

Amanda knew that tone and her heart sank. "Jessica, I knew you would have to uncover more once we got back, but I was hoping you had uncovered most of it before we left."

"Amanda, are you sitting down because this is the bombshell?" Jessica said a little apprehensive.

"Well I am sitting down now and trying to calm myself. So what did you find?" she asked just wanting to get this over with and help her friend move forward with whatever solution she could come up with.

"My wonderful husband of over 23 years has not been employed for 2 years," she said emphatically.

"Two years?" Amanda screamed in disbelief.

"Yes, two years," Jessica said confirming the information.

"You had no idea he wasn't employed?" Amanda said with total confusion.

"Amanda if I knew he wasn't employed all of this shit would make sense now wouldn't it?" she said screaming at what she felt was a rude comment.

"Jessica, I am not judging you. I am just amazed, that's all," she said in a softer tone. She then continued to probe and asked, "So how did you find out?"

"I decided to go to a place in the house I never really go and or pay attention to and that was our basement. I discovered boxes of IRS notices, foreclosure notices, and my ass was not put on notice any of this shit was taking place. I am so pissed right now that I want to kill his ass," she said fuming.

"Jessica, you know I feel your pain. So if he wasn't working, where do you think he was going?"

"Now that is the one million dollar question?" Jessica said not knowing how to even answer that question.

"Well Jess, sit tight and do not let on you know anything. The less you display your disgust for him and put him on notice you might know something, the more leverage you will have."

Turnabout is Fair Play

*"Before you embark on a journey of
revenge, dig two graves."*

— CONFUCIUS

Dick's confirmation of Amanda taking his money infuriated him, but he calmed himself down and turned towards his shield that had protected him through his temporary struggle, his Bible. He took great pride in his new found faith. He had made a personal commitment to stay diligent with his daily readings and attempt to live by what he was taking in. As he casually walked towards the kitchen, he placed his Bible on the granite countertop and turned to Mark 9:23 and read aloud, "And Jesus said to him, if you can, all things are possible for one who believes." He believed one day he would walk again. That happened. So he knew in his mind how God worked and he believed whatever was going to happen, it would be bestowed on Amanda on what He had planned for her. As these thoughts brought a smile to his face, his doorbell rang. Totally caught off guard not anticipating any visitors, he peeked out of his plantation shutters and saw Jacob's car. He pondered should he rush to get in his wheelchair, or should he come clean with Jacob. He wasn't ready for the great reveal. As the doorbell rang again, he got into his wheelchair and made it to the door before Jacob started to return to his car.

"Jacob, sorry it took me so long to get to the door. I wasn't expecting you," Dick said.

"Sorry I popped over unannounced Doc, but I was in the area and just wanted to see how you were doing. It is taking a little longer than anticipated for you to see the group I was telling you about," Jacob said apologetically.

"Hey man, don't worry about it," Dick said as he decided to give Jacob a demonstration on his progress. He had on his shower shoes and decided to wiggle his toes and slightly move his feet.

Jacobs eyes could not believe what he was seeing and said, "This is absolutely amazing. You got anything else you are able to do Doc?"

And without hesitation, he grasped both hands on the side of his wheelchair and stood up.

*   *   *

Amanda received a call from Stevie that he was in town and wanted to meet.

"Amanda I am here in Dallas. I am staying at the Four Points Resort. Are you able to meet me here?" he said hoping she was available.

"Why am I not surprised you decided to stay there of all places?" she said being a little sarcastic.

"Well pretty lady you know I only like the best," he said insinuating not only staying at the best hotel, but he had always thought she was the best.

"Yes, Stevie, I think I can. I just have to make sure I have someone to look after Ryan. I can be there in about an hour if that is okay?" she said not knowing if that was the right place to meet him.

Once she checked in with Ryan, she forgot he had a school project he and a classmate were working on and they had already made arrangements for Ryan to stay over and go to school together the next day, so she had that covered. It had been years since she had been to the resort. When she was married to Dick, they had a membership to the club attached to the resort. She use to workout, play tennis, dine there with her friends, go to the spa, and would occasionally bump into all kind of celebrities from athletes, musicians, and actors coming in and out of the high profile resort.

As she arrived to valet park, the valet recognized her and said, "Welcome back Mrs. Casey. I haven't seen you in…I really can't remember how long, but so glad you are back and what a beautiful car that matches your beautiful smile!"

"Thank you so much Romero. I can't believe you still remember me. It has been a few years since I have been here," Amanda said trying to make small talk.

"Mrs. Casey you have always been so kind and a pleasure to see. Glad to have you back," Romero said proudly.

"Well thank you for remembering me, but, Romero, it's just Ms. Now," Amanda commented with a wink.

"My apologies. I thought you looked lighter. I didn't realize you'd freed yourself from the ball and chain," he said with a cordial blank stare.

"I'll take that as a compliment. You have a good evening," Amanda said trying to leave her vehicle quickly all the while thinking even the valet was privy to Dick's playground.

As she entered the hotel, she saw Stevie in the distance at the bar.

His back was towards her, and she swiftly approached him her frontal torso touching his back as she put her hands over his eyes. She whispered in his ear, "Thank you my knight in shining amour."

Stevie knew that voice, turned around and hugged Amanda like it was going to be the last time seeing her.

"Hey pretty lady. Are you okay?" he said with his eyes gleaming at her presence.

"I am now, and really glad to see you," she said as she returned the hug. She sat down beside him and he ordered her a glass of Chardonnay.

"Amanda are you sure you are okay?" Stevie said knowing the answer.

"For now and seeing you, I know I am okay," she said nervously.

"You know I was hot when you told me you were being followed, and whoever it is, they are going to regret it," he said as if he were ready for battle.

Amanda smiled a sigh of relief as she drank her glass of wine and casually leaned over and hugged Stevie. That was the hug Stevie never thought he would get and he reciprocated.

There was a long period of silence and then Amanda said, "Can we get out of here?"

Stevie could not believe what he was hearing and said, "Ms. Amanda, I have you already taken care of."

* * * *

Amanda woke up a little groggy, but very happy. When she tried to get of out of the fluffy feather bed, she couldn't. There were four dozen red roses surrounding her from the hotel room nightstands, coffee table, and rose petals on top of the duvet. The smell and aroma were overwhelming.

"You up to having breakfast or I guess it's brunch since it is almost noon? I ordered room service thinking you might be a little hungry," Stevie said proudly as he placed a fork of fruit towards her mouth.

She was shell shocked when he announced that she had slept so long. She had no idea she slept so late, and slept like a baby. Opening her mouth, she swallowed the fruit, and grabbed both of his hands. He kissed both of her hands, looked into her eyes and kissed her. Her instincts kicked in and she grabbed his head and kissed him back. Stevie could not believe what was happening, but he definitely was not going to complain. He pulled Amanda away gently and said, "Amanda, do you know what you are doing?" she did not respond and kissed him again passionately never wanting to let go.

Amanda could not believe what had come over her showing more than affection to Stevie. Her actions had clearly muddied the waters and she knew Stevie was where he wanted to be with her. Did she go too far because she was upset with Landon? In hindsight, it was too late to rethink, reset, or undo last night. As she sat up in bed, she enjoyed the fact that Stevie was a quiet sleeper. He was either very satisfied, or at peace. No snoring thank god. She jumped into the shower and put on her clothes she presented with. Stevie fell into an intoxicated sleep as she showered. She leaned over to kiss him goodbye and he woke up.

"You leaving me so soon?" he said disappointed.

"I have to get home half of the day is over, but when I get settled I will call you," she said confused about the previous evening, the ease of their interaction, and how safe he made her feel.

Stevie grabbed Amanda and they both lost control again. He was lost in his want of her, and she lost in the wonderfully thoughtless serenity he provided to her where she could forget Landon, Dick, and her many other worries. In this moment, she was simply in the arms of the man that saved her. More than once she might add.

"Knowledge is a rope, and you're weaving a noose out of it. Leave some slack for the enemy."

— NENIA CAMPBELL, CEASE AND DESIST
(THE IMA, #4)

J essica stayed up waiting for David to get home so she could see his face. So she could feel his deception. He stayed out later than she expected and he wasn't expecting her to be awake. He walked in the door tip toed to not startle anyone in the house and Jessica said, "Good evening, David."

He jumped out of his skin like he had seen a ghost.

"Damn Jess, you scared me," David said slightly frightened and pissed she was still awake because he had to be on his game to answer questions.

"Sorry, I didn't mean to scare you, but you sure are home late," she said ready to bite his head off.

"I couldn't find the plans and went on a wild goose chase and found them finally," David said lying without conviction.

"Are you hungry? I can warm up some food for you," Jessica said wishing she was more on top of her game to put anti-freeze in the food she prepared for him.

"No babe, I grabbed a chicken sandwich in the drive thru," he said even though he had something else to eat.

"Well I am glad you made it home safely," Jessica said as she made her way to their bedroom to go to sleep and figure out her next move and waiting on his. As she tossed and turned through the night not getting any sleep, she wanted to call Amanda, but couldn't risk David discovering she was on to his bullshit and his lies. As David was in a deep snore, she quietly rolled out of the bed and went downstairs. Pacing in the kitchen trying to control her disgust and anger, she decided she had to call Amanda before she did something stupid.

"Hello Stevie?" Amanda said as the phone rang waking her up from her dream reliving their romantic encounter.

"No Amanda it's me Jess," she said slightly frantic and confused she mentioned Stevie.

"Hey Jess, are you alright?" Amanda rubbed her eyes to wake herself up.

"Yes and no," Jessica whispered and cupped her hand around her mouth and the phone in an effort to not be overheard.

"You have me concerned. Why are you whispering?"

"David is here and Amanda I cannot sleep next to him knowing what I know. This is too difficult for me to keep in without exploding. He had the nerve to come home late as if he were working late. I can't take this shit. Please help me," Jessica said with desperation.

"Jessica, I know this is hard, but you have to play like everything is fine. Please trust me when I say this."

"Okay, okay," Jessica continued to whisper.

"Jessica put on your best 'Betty Crocker' act and keep this shit moving until we can figure out your next move. Please promise me you will do this."

"Thanks Amanda. I just needed that extra push to keep me in line. This is so hard, but I am listening and will talk to you tomorrow," Jess said struggling to keep her composure under so much duress.

As every woman does at some point in her life, Jessica took a couple deep breaths and set her focus on the task at hand. She returned to the master bedroom and put herself to bed – even if it was at the very farthest edge. Jessica finally fell asleep, but it was hardly enough sleep to keep her in the right frame of mind. As Amanda had instructed, Jessica woke up as if nothing was wrong. She made her boys and David breakfast and kept to her normal routine. Well almost normal except for dropping some of the pancakes on the kitchen floor that made her boys laugh hysterically, and made David want to help her out, which she resisted.

"Thanks David, but I got this," Jessica said with anger.

"Jess, I was just trying to help," David said.

With the boys' incessant laughter and David pretending to be the doting father, she almost slapped the shit out of David with the spatula, but missed.

"So David, what time will you be home this evening?" Jessica said as if she was concerned.

"I'm not sure, but I will call you midday and let you know," he said not noticing she was on to him.

*   *   *

Jacob could not keep his mouth closed and looked as if his mind was playing tricks on him when he saw what Dr. Casey displayed.

"Pretty shocking isn't it?" Dick said with a sinister smile on his face.

"It's more than shocking, I guess my next question is what is our next step because this is a game changer," Jacob said perplexed.

"Well I have done some research and I want to continue my physical therapy to continue strengthening my limbs and at some point get confirmation that I am well on my way to recovery," Dick said with his usual cockiness.

"Well I think that is a great plan and we will continue with your care and I am excited to work with you and see more of your progress," Jacob said grinning from ear to ear.

* * *

Anxiety had set in with Amanda's unexpected triste with Stevie, confusion with her relationship with Landon, and Jessica's challenges with David. It was too much to handle. She needed to recycle her focus and decided that she would pick Ryan up from school and take him to get his favorite, Sushi.

"I thought Mini was picking me up today?" Ryan said with his lip poked out.

"Oh so you're not happy to see me?" Amanda stated happy to see him.

"Of course I am mom, I was just hoping Mini was picking me up because it's Friday and she had promised to take me to that Fast and Furious movie."

"Well you can do that tomorrow or even Sunday. I just wanted to spend some time with you and take you to Hana Sushi to catch up, if that's okay," she said happy to be in his company.

"We haven't been to Hana Sushi in a long time," he said excited that they were going. With all of the financial limitations they had and not being able to do some of the things they use to do, he was excited as well.

"I know so I thought we could treat ourselves to those Mt. Fuji Rolls, Texas Tornado Rolls, and your usual, Shrimp Fried Rice," she said with a smile.

We were greeted by a familiar face, Tina. Her face lit up when she saw us and ran to Ryan and gave him a big hug.

"You got taller. You are a big boy now!" she said as if she was going to cry.

Ryan let Tina know, "Well I am 14 now," he said with pride.

"Fourteen. You driving a car now?" she said jokingly.

"Not yet, but I can't wait," Ryan said knowing his Mini had been teaching him how to drive at her church parking lot since he was twelve without Amanda's knowledge.

"We have missed you. How have you been?"

Tina's face was showing signs of some relief.

"We are doing just fine now," Amanda said wondering why Tina was acting that way.

Before Tina seated them, she whispered in Amanda's ear with her cute Asian accent, "I saw that doctor husband with another woman a few times here. She was a ugly lady in here and out here," Tina motioned with her right finger towards her heart, and gestured with her left hand rubbing her face. It was her way of explaining to me the woman she saw was ugly inside and outside.

"I did not know what was happening. It made me sad and I did not want to talk to him when he would come in with her," she said a bit provoked.

"Tina, it is fine and I appreciate your ability to see through that cheating ex-husband that I divorced," Amanda said wanting to laugh.

Tina continued to gossip at a whisper, "But I don't see him in here with her anymore," she said wanting to know why.

"It's probably because he is not in a good place right now, but no need to worry about him anymore," Amanda said like her mission was accomplished.

"Well, I am happy you are back," she said as she smiled with her eyes.

We sat down and it was like old times. Then out of the blue "Mister Nosey" asked me, "Mom, what was it Tina was saying to you she couldn't say in front of me?"

"Just stuff about Dick you didn't need to hear," Amanda said ready to order.

"Mom, I knew Dick was banging Ed Ballard's girlfriend Suzanne. Everyone at school knew that," Ryan said very cavalier.

Amanda felt flushed and thought she was going to faint after hearing his comment. Ryan had never mentioned anything about what happened in the divorce. All she wanted to do now was eat, but he continued his synopsis of the situation and offered this, "Mom you are and we are better off without him. I know some of the stunts he pulled, and I didn't like it. I thought at some point he would stop. I even felt sorry for him now he is in that wheelchair, but now, I don't. I sure hope he has learned his lesson."

As he ended his speech, Tina came over to take their order and boy was she relieved. The time was well spent with Ryan, eating their favorite Sushi Rolls, and laughing about some of the silly girls that like him at school, and boy it was like pulling teeth to pry out that information. She was happy to hear he enjoyed where they were living and glad they were not living the way they were previously in that beautiful home with electric, water, and cable at times being cut off because Dick refused to pay the bills. Oh, how could she forget the summer one of the air conditioner units had gone out the first year of going through the divorce, and the following winter when one of the heating units had gone out and she had to beg him to get them fixed. She was ashamed that her attorney had to get involved to get the air and heat back on. Her heart was dancing to see Ryan smile about their new place. It made her feel appreciated even though he had no idea everything she really had to go through. She had to protect him from that after all he was only fourteen going on thirty in mere seconds.

Dormant Storm

"She can only take so much, she has been bottling her emotions, she is about to break. This is the calm before the storm."

— UNKNOWN

J essica allowed David a pass by letting him out the door to go to his so called job. While he was pretending to have legitimate employment, she decided to do what Amanda suggested. She started to make calls to find out how much was owed on the house, taxes, and day to day utilities that were at risk to be disconnected. Flustered and frustrated with it all she needed to do she called Amanda and had one big question to ask her.

"Hello Jess. What's up?" Amanda said cautiously.

"I called to let you know am gathering up all the information you and I discussed so you can let me know where to go from here," Jessica sounded very businesslike.

"Now that's a start. I'm so glad you are getting all of that together."

"Amanda, can I ask you something?" Jessica said puzzled.

"Sure Jess. You are sounding really serious. What do you need to ask me?" Amanda said taken aback that she was deflecting what was going on with her in another direction.

"When I called you last night, you thought I was Stevie. Why was that?"

She said not really ready for the response.

Amanda paused for a while and then offered, "I met with him because someone was following me the other night and he is in town to see if Dick is coming after me," she said slightly embarrassed.

"You mean to tell me someone has been following you?" Jessica said upset.

"Jess, you have so much going on that I refuse to add to your stress level, but yes some crazy was following me after my dinner with Landon," Amanda said frustrated.

"And speaking of Landon, I have not heard you mention his name at all. Are you two in a good place?"

Jessica said like she was the therapist turning the table around on Amanda.

Amanda's acting skills were lacking as she tried to look to the side to guide her tears another direction, but she wasn't fast enough and tears began to roll down her face.

"Amanda we are good friends. I can hear those tears through this phone. What is going on that you are not sharing with me?" Jessica demanded to know.

"Jess if you must know the short version is Landon has a crazy ass ex-girlfriend stalker type he thought was out of his life, but the bitch has reappeared."

"What a shit show Amanda! I hate men even more. Landon is a good guy. He's not seeing her is he?" Jessica said needing clarification.

"No, but he seemed like he felt sorry for her, and that my dear is going to be a problem. That means he can't let go or put her where she needs to be which is in the past," Amanda said with conviction.

"Amanda, I felt like he was the one after that psycho ass Dick Casey," she said angrily.

"Jess, don't worry about me, but please get all the information you need and be very careful not to let

David find out. You never know how these men will react when they are found out," Amanda said as the expert in this situation.

*　*　*

Amanda had peace and quiet to herself for a change. She cooked for Ryan as he was doing homework, but that was going to be short lived. Her phone rang and the contact name was Landon. She wasn't sure to pick it up or let it go to voicemail. Her reflexes said otherwise and she took the call with the uncertainty of where the conversation would go.

"Hello."

Amanda said half afraid because of the end of their evening after the car incident.

"Amanda I miss you immensely. How can we fix this?" Landon said wanting everything he told her previously to go away.

"Landon I don't know, but what I do know is after you told me about your ex, Nikki, I was followed and managed to get rid of them," she said with a slight attitude he had never heard before.

He was hesitant after hearing her exchange and finally was brave enough to say, "My love, I hate that my past has interfered with our present, but rest assured, I will take care of it," Landon said with the upmost conviction.

In Amanda's mind, it was too late. She had given her body and her trust to Stevie and trust was huge because Stevie delivered past, present, and maybe future. She was smart enough to keep that under wraps and responded to Landon, "It seems like she is a bit much and I hope she wasn't the one following me."

Landon immediately came back, which is so not like him, and said, "Are you sure it was not your ex-husband, Dick?" he said with confidence.

"Landon, it could be one of the two, but they both add to my stress level."

"I totally understand Amanda and I want to protect you from any more hurt you have already had to endure," Landon said heartfelt.

Amanda's heart was crushed because she believed him. Maybe she rushed her feelings with Stevie because Landon sprung up the crazy ex.

"There are no secrets that time does not reveal."

— Jean Racine

Jacob was totally astonished that Dr. Casey had more mobility than displayed during his previous therapy sessions. The smile on his face said it all. Dick on the other hand, happy the secret found its way to the surface instead of showboating with a big reveal. It was time to get on with what really mattered to him; that was getting what Amanda deserved. Let's be clear, not by his hands, but by someone else, Him. He knew God was on his side. After entertaining Jacob with his Cirque de Soleil show, he walked towards his nightstand in his bedroom to read his Bible. He conveniently turned to Psalm 118:6-9.

He read aloud smiling, "The Lord is on my side; I will not fear. What can man do to me? The Lord is on my side as my helper; I shall look in triumph on those who hate me. It is better to take refuge in the Lord than to trust in man. It is better to take refuge in the Lord than to trust the princes." After reading the Psalm, he found it fitting to call Lenny to make sure he was doing his due diligence to find Taylor. He was ready to see her now that he escaped the wrath of eternal confinement to his circumstance, the wheelchair.

He dialed Lenny and as Lenny answered his call he yelled, "Hey man, have you found my princess?"

"Doc I have found her and I apologize for not calling you sooner, but I didn't know how to tell you," Lenny said.

"Tell me what?" Dick said.

"I hate to deliver this bad news, but she has her eyes on someone else, and it isn't you," Lenny said very hesitant.

"Talk to me man. I am listening," Dick said pissed off.

"Doc, she is into this personal training shit and works out with a trainer and that dude I don't think he even knows she is into him, but she follows him. One night she was parked outside a restaurant I guess he was dining there by himself or with someone I don't know, because I couldn't see that well and trying to keep my eye on Taylor she took off so fast I couldn't catch up with her," he said too embarrassed to share that information.

"So she is in a relationship with this trainer?" Dick questioned.

"Doc she is in her mind, because I don't think this dude knows," Lenny said with his latest Intel.

"Find out who this trainer is for me, and keep up with Ms. Taylor Park," Dick said pissed that she had made up her mind to set her sights on someone else and he was clearly an afterthought. Everything he had done for her to get her out of a bad situation with a husband that was a drunk and beat her. How he would listen endlessly to her torment instead of discussing how he was going to treat her melanoma. He had big plans for the two of them after they would wed. He had already met with a builder to build their dream home and this is how she treats him.

* * *

Jessica got everything she needed for Amanda to help her out of the mess David had created for her and the boys, but she still wasn't feeling any relief. She felt evil was lurking, but she did not know where it was coming from. She felt she should start with the so called "other family". She needed to find out what David also had his hands into that needed to be divulged and if it had included her sister Julie. She decided to find out for herself so she called her nemesis sister Julie.

"Hello." Julie answered.

"Hey Sis, I haven't heard from you in a while. What's going on?" Jessica said inquisitively.

"Well this is a pleasant surprise. I rarely hear from you. So what is going on?" Julie said without a care in the world.

"To be honest, that's why I am calling you. I haven't seen you at any of the boy's activities lately so I was checking in to see if you were alright. You are one of their biggest cheerleaders," Jessica said in an endearing way.

"Well don't worry about me Jess. I am perfectly fine," she said a bit condescending.

Trying to continue to make small talk Jessica asked her, "Have you spoken to Debra lately?"

"No can't say I have," she said sounding a bit annoyed. And then the real reason Jessica was calling found its way into the pedestrian conversation, "Have you seen David?"

"That's your husband Jessica, not mine. You can't keep up with your own man?" she said with a chuckle.

Jessica was fuming and announced, "Julie you are my sister. Why you act like you are my enemy is beyond comprehension? Good bye."

Julie's attempt to utter another word was short lived because Jessica abruptly hung up the phone. She was caught off guard when Jessica asked her if she had spoken to Debra and then segued into asking where her own husband was. Julie started pacing back and forth in her bedroom making lines in the carpet as if her feet were the vacuum cleaner to clean up dirt on the floor. Wondering if Jessica was fishing for information or somehow she found out the real dirt that she was sleeping with Debra's husband, William.

"If you want the naked beauty of my vulnerability, you have to have the strength to share the burden of, the private pain, that makes me feel so tender and fragile. For I am as strong, as I am, weak. If you want me to come home to you, be the safe harbor, in which, I can seek refuge."

— JAEDA DEWALT

The warrior, the protector, the end all of everything, the lover, were the traits Amanda thought Landon possessed, but as of late, it was all displayed by Stevie. Yes Landon was the distraction she needed during her haring divorce and was there for her to comfort, but Stevie did the work to save her from financial ruin and now somehow he has her heart, or does he. Confusion set in and she didn't know which direction to go. The resurgence of Landon's ex-girlfriend led to the waters getting muddied and her seeking refuge with Stevie. Contemplating on calling him to see where his head was, her telepathic skills made her cellphone ring and the contact was Stevie.

"Hello," she said hesitantly.

"Amanda did you lose your humor? I didn't even get 'I1MYWAY' how can I help you," Stevie said with a chuckle.

"Sorry Stevie, I have a lot on my mind and trying to help my friend Jess," Amanda said hoping he wasn't able to read more into her demeanor.

"Your wish is my command pretty lady. You need my help."

Amanda started to focus, ran this offer through her head, and said, "Yes I do. I need your expertise again of finding out the truth on Jessica's husband David. David Scott, project manager for Z Corp his last employment stint. The perpetrator drives a blue BMW X6 SUV."

"That's not a problem baby. You know I don't need a complete resume to scratch the surface on what this dude is up to. If I need anything else, I will let you know," he said more than happy to oblige.

There was an unexpected long pause after that exchange.

Breaking the silence, Stevie mustered up the courage and said, "Amanda, I really enjoyed our time together. I know you have alluded to some uncertainty with where you and Landon are and I hope that didn't make you sleep with me."

That comment was direct and to the point which clouded Amanda's vision. She did not know how to respond not wanting to say the wrong thing. Seeking refuge with Stevie was more than exhilarating. Taking her to a place she had never been before, not even with Landon. It was erotic and hypnotic. It started when she hugged him at the bar and the smell of his neck wafting scent of apple and currants with a hint of smoky jasmine and vanilla. She was familiar with that expensive cologne, Creed Aventus, and it was mesmerizing. His sensual touch escalated once they arrived at his hotel room. His soft kisses and neck massage led to every inch of her body getting the same treatment. At that point, there was no turning back. There were no thoughts of Landon, just Stevie's Midas touch.

* * *

Julie was sweating like she was way past her menopausal days, and at the age of 60, she was. Still attractive at her age, but back in her day, she turned heads. She was drop dead gorgeous and she knew it. You couldn't tell her she wasn't a big deal, and she lived her life like that. Everything she did was over the top and she could afford to do so because she was married to a NBA player. That was short lived after his philandering ways and eventually a career ending injury that also was the precursor to the end of their marriage. She always needed stability and comfort and maybe that's why she sought refuge pursing a married man, her sister's husband, William. William was a real estate developer and took care of his wife, Debra, very well. Julie had to contact William to give him a heads up that their secret may be exposed.

"Hey Julie, you sound upset," William said.

"I am more than upset. I think that stupid ass sister of mine, Jessica, knows something," she said apprehensively.

"She knows what honey?" William questioned.

"I think she knows we are seeing each other. It was bizarre. She never calls me, and then out of the blue she called and asked a lot of questions including asking about that no good husband of hers, David. I know David's secret, and I have protected him as he knows ours," she said sounding afraid.

"Don't worry about it. I will make sure that doesn't happen," William said.

Of course he would make sure that would not happen. He had a lot to lose.

*"I'm telling you this because I want you
to know that I know something about
you isn't right. You have fooled everybody.
I'm going to find out what you're up to.
I'm going to expose you."*

— BECCA FITZPATRICK
HUSH, HUSH (HUSH, HUSH, #1)

Now that Dick's new found agility had been exposed to Jacob, it's time for the great reveal and sharing the good news with Lenny and to get the plan in action for Amanda's new situation that was being concocted for her.

"Hey Lenny are you available to stop by? I have some plans I need to review with you," Dick said with an authoritative tone.

"Sure Doc. Just give me an hour and I can be right there. You okay?" Lenny said a bit uncomfortable not knowing his fate or what Dick has planned for him.

"Man I am more than alright. I will see you when you get here."

Dick prepared for the unveiling. He put on his best Robert Graham shirt and dark denim jeans, and Gucci loafers. Looking at his wheelchair at a distance triumphantly, he was ready to go the distance to win and get Taylor and his money back. He took his hands and pressed them down his shirt to make sure it was perfectly smooth without wrinkles. The doorbell rang and Dick strolled slowly to the door his hand reaching for the doorknob just as slowly as if he were approaching Taylor trying to take her hand. As he opened the door, the look on Lenny's face was priceless. He looked as if he had seen his dead father.

Stuttering he said, "Doc, doc you are walking. When did this happen?"

"Man I'm a fighter and I knew this shit was temporary and I would walk again," Dick said with more confidence he had ever displayed.

"It's a miracle man. I'm happy for you," Lenny said elated, but his face said it all. He was afraid, very afraid now that Dick was walking. Lenny knew any one that crossed his path and betrayed him had hell to pay.

"Lenny you said you are happy, but your face says otherwise. What's up?" Dick said in a very sneaky tone.

"Nothing man, just still in shock. That's all," Lenny said lying understanding the gravity of any slipups this time would be the end of him.

"Well let's get down to business," Dick shouted. He patted Lenny on the back and held his hand there as he ushered Lenny in the door and into the living room.

Thoughts consumed Lenny's head, but he knew he owed Dick and had to make things right, which was depressing after feeling hope brush across his heart. As long as Dick was in the wheelchair, Lenny didn't have to worry as much about his role in Dick's plans and if he abandoned his post there wasn't much Dick could do to him. Walking returned power to this once fallen king and his reign would gain power by the day. Something's not right with this world if people like Dick keep winning.

* * *

Stevie took in everything Amanda shared with him and started his investigation with Landon to find out who could possibly be following her. His gut told him to start with Landon since he was the most recent source of harm to Amanda and maybe he also wanted to check out the competition. As he started his assignment to uncover Landon's whereabouts, he unexpectedly got his first piece of information on what may be going on. As he sat outside where Landon trained his clients, he noticed a client that looked quite familiar from a description Amanda shared awhile back about Dick's penchant for redheads. After Landon would leave the club, this particular client hung around and began to follow him. He took the plate number and where this person lived and low and behold, her name was Taylor Park. She was Dick's girl. Why was she following Landon? Only time would tell, but Stevie was now keeping a watchful eye on Ms. Taylor Park.

*　*　*

One evening when David was out of the house yet again for some mysterious work event and the boys were off at friends, Jessica called Amanda and the two of them reviewed all the facts and figures Jess had uncovered. Amanda asked a bunch of questions and asked to see the documents. Since they were Face Timing, they spoke at length covering each document. Amanda was satisfied with the information Jessica provided her and reassured her friend that she would not lose her house or be in the house in silence and darkness. Darkness always comes to light, so the next lie and secret that needed to be uncovered was the one David was living. That wouldn't be too hard with Stevie on the case.

Amanda wanted to keep her relationship with Stevie businesslike, but it was too late for that. It was uncomfortable now to call him to get updates on David because, yes, she wanted to get what she needed to help Jessica, and at the same time, she had caught feelings for Stevie. That night at the hotel still resonated in her mind, and confusion was at its upmost threshold. Stevie made her forget everything that was surrounding her reality, just like Landon did in the beginning. But between the two there was a difference and there will be a time where she needed to decide who she wanted to share her future with. Without giving her room to breathe her phone rang and it was Landon. She did not want to let on anything was wrong, but definitely wanted to see what sand box he was playing in.

"Hey babe, I miss you. What's going on with you? We seem a bit disconnected," Landon said sadly.

"No Landon we are not, but you know I am a bit consumed with helping Jessica out of her mess," she said as if she was dodging a bullet.

"Amanda it has been way too long since we have even been together. Is Nikki the problem?" he asked like it wasn't an issue.

"To be honest Landon, she is an issue and I don't see you making her a non-issue," Amanda said emphatically.

"Amanda, I am not used to someone fussing at me and especially when it is not the case."

Although this dismissal of her opinion and perspective miffed her, she responded calmly with, "Landon please I am not fussing, but I expect some respect."

"I respect you Amanda. What are you talking about?" he said angrily and clearly not understanding the issue.

"Nikki is the disrespect I am talking about," she said intentionally picking a fight after hearing his anger.

"She is a non-factor Amanda. Please let's just meet. I want to see you," he said longing for her affection.

Struggling with her feelings and feeling like a liar and a cheater, like Dick Casey, was killing her inside. She didn't want to be that type of person and it wasn't easy because it wasn't in her character, but she couldn't muster up any truthful explanation of how she felt to Landon. Not now anyway. She decided to procrastinate the inevitable conversation and diverted her answer with, "I would like to see you too Landon, but I need to tie up these loose ends for my friend. Time is crucial right now and there are some other issues that need attention and I have not tackled those yet for her."

That was a mouthful and she thought it was convincing, until Landon said, "No worries Amanda. I get it. You don't want to see me," he played the pity card.

"Landon, really I have a lot going on and you and I have a lot to hash out," she said sternly not letting him have the pity.

"Oh so now it's hashing out," Landon wasn't giving up his argument.

"I am not going to dance back and forth with you right now. Please be patient with me as I have been with you. I have a call coming in I need to answer. I will call you tomorrow," she said totally being untruthful, but tired of the tango conversation going nowhere. It was moments like this when grown men acted like babies that she weighed even having a man in her life. Then again they were fun as the thought of Stevie's touch sent a flash of desire through her. The scale with the two men on it just tipped again.

Landon lay in his empty bed astonished. How could she not understand that Nikki was in the past even though he still wished her well and that Amanda was his future? He dropped to the floor and did several push-ups and crunches to work out his frustration.

By Any Means Necessary

:by doing whatever is needed
:to design for or destine to a specified

— PURPOSE OR FUTURE
MERRIAM-WEBSTER

D ick would go to the end of the earth to get Taylor back and to put Amanda in her place. His anticipation of taking down Amanda and taking Taylor back created a natural high. He was excited, adrenalin rushing, but he needed to slow down not to make any mistakes like the last time. Lenny had gone above and beyond to help Dick, even without any local help from Vernon Mack. The feedback Lenny received from his boys indicated Vernon Mack's existence may come to an end soon, and Lenny did not want to become a member of that club. He did not illicit anymore of Vernon's help with this new assignment. He knew he had to do it on his own. Lenny and Dick met on several occasions plotting and planning their next moves.

On the other front, Stevie was plotting and planning as well. Now that he was on to Taylor, he knew Dick wasn't far out of sight. Stevie's gut told him even though Dick was in that wheelchair, that he could still be dangerous. He decided to do more investigating beginning with Lenny since he was so easy to track down the last time. He didn't want to alarm Amanda, so he kept his plan under wraps. The chess game ensued. Stevie thought it best to start at the beginning, which was Dick's old office. As he camped out at Dick's office hoping something would provide him a clue, the devil surfaced walking like on a catwalk of Fashion Week in New York. It was more than Stevie could handle. A black Range Rover pulled up and out of that vehicle was Lucifer himself. Pulling off his Ray Ban shades and looking around to make sure he had dodged the paparazzi, it was Dick walking into his office. Stevie couldn't believe his eyes and wanted to call Amanda, but he knew that shit would spook her. That definitely was not what he was expecting. He picked up his cellphone and dialed Neko.

"Hey man what's up? Neko answered.

"A lot. I need you to get to Dallas quickly," Stevie said slightly out of breath.

"Shit sounds serious. What's up?" Neko said willing and ready.

"Man I don't want to scare the shit out of Amanda, but that crazy ass ex-husband that was in a wheelchair, is flossing in a Range Rover walking faster than me and you put together," Stevie said in disbelief.

"What? You have got to be kidding me! What magician did he find to change his circumstance? Man you know the dudes we ran with that got shot and ended up in a chair never got to put two feet on the ground moving forward," Neko was so astonished by the news he rambled on a bit.

"I know. I'm telling you this dude is walking and he is dangerous. I know he has it in for Amanda, so we have to beat him to the punch," Stevie said very protective like and laced with anxiety.

"Man I see how you look at Amanda and how you really feel about her. I am on my way. You took care of me, man, and I know you want to take care of her," Neko said reminiscing and completely understanding where his best friend and business partner was coming from. Neko had an experience or two with a female worth doing anything for and Stevie was always there to lend a hand.

Stevie kept his eye on Dick and low and behold another car pulled up and it was Lenny. This was Stevie's lucky day. Lenny's presence was all the confirmation he needed for he and Neko to keep Amanda protected. He had most of the pieces together with Taylor, Dick, and Lenny. What he needed to find out was who was following Amanda and why? He had good instincts, but he needed to know for a fact who that individual could be and, if it wasn't one of the key suspects, which one of them hired the lackey.

*　　*　　*

Jessica was so thankful for Amanda's generosity and now she was ready to put David on notice. Julie's evasive posture provided nothing she could put her finger on, but the conversation pulled the tension tighter in her already tethering patience. She had hoped her sister would provide her with some clue as to what her unemployed husband was doing and where he could be spending his time. To get the ball rolling, she called Amanda to take her up on her main resource for getting answers and getting a job done, Stevie.

Amanda's cellphone rang and she saw the call was from Jess. "Hey Jess is everything okay and are the boys alright?"

"Yes we are fine, but I am calling to see if Stevie is available to find out what David is up to? And with that information what should be my next step?" Jessica said ready to go to war.

"I have shared just a small piece of information on David with Stevie and will follow up on his findings. Based on my experience Jess, Stevie can find out anything and then you know what your next step is going to be," Amanda said firmly and confidently.

Jessica sighed, "I know Amanda and that is something I am not ready to face yet. Let's take this one step at a time and find out what the hell David has been up to and why he has us in this mess, if that's okay with you."

"No worries. I will give Stevie a call. He has been upset by someone following me and I know he is trying to get to the bottom of it as we speak. I will call you when we get the information that is needed and you still need to maintain your composure and keep your acting skills at an all-time high. You cannot afford to slip up and David find out you know he is a snake. You got it Jessica?" Amanda said as if she was scolding her own son Ryan.

"Yes, ma'am. I got it Amanda. Thanks honey. What would I do without you?" Jessica said as she hung up to Amanda laughing at her response.

Jessica was comfortable with Stevie as her investigator, but she couldn't help herself; she decided to do some of her own investigating by calling David to maybe catch him off guard. If he slips up, she could use that to solve the puzzle.

"Hello," David answered hesitantly.

"Hi, David, I was just checking in and wanted to know if you could pick the boys up from practice after work," Jessica said anticipating what lie he would tell.

David quickly answered, "Awe babe, I wish I could, but I have a meeting that may run late. Can you still pick them up?"

"I can. I just thought you might leave work early and go watch them and bring them home like you used to."

"I wish I could, and once this project is over I will resume picking them up like old times," he calmly explained all the while perspiring profusely.

She wasn't taking a detour with his false promise and stayed on course. Jessica was so frustrated she almost blurted out "I know you are unemployed," but she kept Amanda's advice in her head and told him, "I guess we will see you when you get home."

"See you later," David said not knowing how long he could continue the façade. When he hung up he exhaled the breath that was caught in his chest every time he interacted with her these days.

Jessica was not going to give up so easily; she was determined to find out her husband's lies by any means necessary.

My Prerogative

"I don't need permission
Make my own decisions
That's my prerogative"

— Bobby Brown
My Prerogative Lyrics

Dr. Richard Casey was back in full force. This time there would be no hiccups. Lenny had been briefed on his continued surveillance on Taylor and also Amanda. Yes, Lenny was still working on finding out where Amanda lived, but had a feeling that was not where the money was he was sure of it; she is smarter than that.

Unbeknownst to them, they were not the only ones wanting answers. Stevie was not going to let Amanda come into harm's way and he and Neko were ready to protect her. Neko arrived in Dallas and he and Stevie devised their plan. Neko wanted Dick Casey put in his place as much as Stevie so he shared with Stevie that he enlisted some local help that he felt were good soldiers for this job. Dick, Lenny, Taylor, Stevie, and Neko let the games begin. Now that Stevie knew about Dick, he had to give Amanda a heads up and quickly. He couldn't speed dial her number fast enough.

He dialed but she didn't answer. Again, he dialed and then it went immediately to voicemail. Worry started to set in and as if a rocket had been launched under the hood of his Mercedes, he was at Amanda's house in no time. Everything seemed normal as he pulled up. He rang the doorbell and no one answered. He was on the verge of losing it and walked to the side of the house and opened the gate that led to the back of the home and the pool. And there she was, caramel skin, Chanel shades, Trina Turk tankini lounging by the pool soaking up the sun. Before he could approach her and let her know he was there, he had to regain his composure. He did not want Amanda to see him disheveled totally full of fear that something awful had happened to her. Not to startle her he yelled, "He baby it's me."

She turned quickly recognizing the voice and said, "Stevie, what are you doing here?" she said pleasantly surprised.

"Baby you had me scared shitless. I have been calling you and then your phone went immediately to voicemail and I had this feeling something bad had taken place. Where is your phone?" he said trying his best to maintain some sense of calm.

"Damn, I must have left it on the island in the kitchen and if it went to voicemail then the battery must be dead. I need to charge it quickly just in case Ryan is trying to reach me. He is with his best friend and his family from our old neighborhood in Hot Springs Arkansas. I thought it would do me some good to enjoy my pool and relax after speaking to Jessica, and on that note have your guys found out what her clown of a husband has been up to?"

She walked as she talked to retrieve her phone, plug it in, and turned back to Stevie as she asked her question. She smiled as she caught his eyes coming up her body like his tongue did... Luckily, he spoke before her mind could recall that memory completely.

"Amanda, I am a step ahead of you. One of my guys from the crew, I got him monitoring David's activities and he is efficient, like me, and has already reported back. He said that joker is more than a clown. This dude gets dressed like he is going to an office, but that office is a coffee house every single day for at least four hours."

"A coffee house?" Amanda questioned.

"Yes, and he's not working behind the counter," Stevie added for emphasis and clarity.

Stevie proceeded to tell her that his guy sat next to him but not too close and he was on job sites looking for employment in between visiting porn sights.

Amanda blurted out, "This shit is reminiscent of the behavior of Dr. Richard Casey all over again. What the hell is up with these men and porn sites? I don't know what's worse a drug addiction or addiction to female genitalia."

Stevie chuckled. "Baby it gets even better. You ready for this?" Stevie said waiting for Amanda to brace herself, which she did on her kitchen counter.

"He leaves there and goes to Jessica's sister's house, Julie. It's like clockwork."

"So what you are saying is he and Julie are having an affair?" Amanda said in shock. She really didn't want Jessica to be right on that one, but here it is.

"No, not at all," Stevie shook his head.

"Well if they are not having an affair, why is he going to her house?" Her face scrunched up, utterly confused as to why the two in-laws would hang out every day. No one liked his or her brother or sister in-laws that much.

"Babe he goes there because he doesn't have anywhere else to go, and he gets paid to house sit."

"Housesit, like babysit without the baby?" Amanda said shaking her head.

"Exactly and get this. Julie leaves when he is there and on occasion will go to the Best Western Elite Hotel, or Hotel Inn."

"Well now this shit is sounding very familiar. Someone else mimicking Dick Casey's moves. I can't take anymore," Amanda said exasperated and threw her hands up.

"I'm not finished Amanda. She meets a man at these places named William. Do you know who that is?" Stevie asked not knowing exactly who this person was without digging deeper.

Amanda's hands fell to her sides and she turned pale looking as if she was going to faint. After a beat, she replied, "If it is who I think it is, it's Jessica's sister Debra's husband."

Stevie let that soak in for a second and he hated that he had more bad news for her. However, she needed to know, so he pressed on in a softer tone. "Amanda I am not dismissing what is going on with your friend Jessica right now, but I also need to share some disturbing news and I feel I need to stay close to you. Please don't take this wrong when I say I feel I need to stay here with you and let Neko and his boys get to work."

Amanda just stared at him as he spoke. Her body instinctively went to sit down, like the truths were too much weight for her to carry.

"Stevie you are scaring me. What is it you need to share?"

He watched as she braced her hands on her bare knees and he kneeled to squat in front of her. She was one tough lady, but this was going to hurt and send panic through her.

"Baby as I was trying to uncover who was following you. I decided to start at square one, your ex. I went to his office and..." He couldn't finish his sentence. His instinct to protect her was fighting the fact that he had to tell her.

Amanda visibly upset said, "What is it Stevie?" One of her hands went to his shoulder to shake it out of him.

Staring into her beautiful eyes, willing her to hear this truth, he said, "Baby, Dr. Dick Casey is walking!"

Her nails instantly dug into his flesh, but he refused to wince. Confusion and anger were written all over Amanda's face. She whispered, "He is walking?"

"He wasn't yours to get hurt by. He was someone else's and you knew that, so why are you offended? What right do you have to be hurt when you were a part of the deception (lying by omission)?"

— DONNA LYNN HOPE

Julie was reeling and confused about keeping her secret intact. The one person that knew the secret was David, and as of late, he was not very stable. She was keeping his secret, but who would break first and cross the other. Only time would tell.

Scared and infuriated with the latest exchange with her sister Jessica, Julie decided to be at her home when David arrived at his usual time. As he put the key in the lock and opened the door, he was startled to see her. Their eyes met feeling each other out on who was going to begin their exchange of words and stand their ground on where their fate was headed. It was Julie's home court so she decided to begin the sparing match.

"David, I have covered for your ass for two years. Why you still do not have employment is beyond me, but player, you better hurry up and get your shit together because your wife is going to finally catchup to your bullshit," Julie said extremely pissed off.

"Julie, you trick! How dare you threaten me when you are in on not telling Jessica about her fairytale life that doesn't exist anymore? I have tried to get another job, but the shit is rough out here," he screamed, lashing back at her insult. Walking back and forth pacing the floor he spewed, "And you of all people have the nerve to scrutinize me when not only are you hiding a secret from your sister, Jessica, your fucking your other sister's husband. So slut don't come for me like that," he yelled even louder.

Looking as if she was losing this battle, Julie delivered a scathing statement, "My personal affairs are not causing anyone personal financial strife, but your shit is!"

Like the legendary boxers Ali and Frasier, they continued to deliver their blows and banters and finally David said, "I'm out of here Julie. Watch yourself."

And with that he slammed the door and left. She was glad he left, but now she was more afraid than ever that he would blow her cover.

* * *

Landon's heart was still hurt by Amanda's evasive behavior. Instead of calling her again, he headed out to work and met with his clients in hopes that would keep his mind off of her. As he pulled up in the parking lot, he saw one of his clients, Taylor. She pulled up beside him smiling ear to ear. Landon enjoyed the smile on her face and the feeling of having at least one fine looking female happy to see him.

"Hey Landon. I am ready to get this work out in," she said very giddy.

"Okay Ms. Taylor, I will see you inside," Landon playfully stated.

Once inside the workout began. Landon noticed her fondness of him, but he never paid it much attention nor did he encourage her advances. He thought, "This too shall pass" as he was packing up his gym bag and walking towards his car, Taylor stopped abruptly in front of him.

"Hey Landon where are you headed?" she said inquisitively.

"Oh Taylor, I am just going to run some errands. Why? What's up?" he said a little agitated attempting to get into his car.

"Just wanted to say thanks for the great workout and wanted to know if you were available to grab a bite to eat or maybe a drink?"

"Thanks for the invite, but I have some things I need to attend to. Maybe next time," he said not really meaning it.

"Alright Mr. Landon. Get your errands done," she said flirtatiously. He looked so cute trying to impress her with his important errands. Then again, what errands would be more important than spending time with her?

As Landon sped away from his uncomfortable exchange with Taylor, his thoughts switched to Amanda. Taylor, on the other hand, did not take kindly to Landon's rejection. She longed for Landon the way she fell for Dr. Richard Casey. She loved the attention

Dick gave her, but she had difficulty returning it after his misfortune in the courtroom and ending up in that hideous wheelchair. Being a caregiver was not in her plans. They had planned on spending their life together traveling and enjoying one another; however, she couldn't accept the fate that changed her and Dick's life forever. She had so much more to live for and felt her only option was to leave him and start her life all over again. And indeed she welcomed a fresh start. Her fresh start began with a personal makeover. She came out of her ordinary looking cocoon, but kept her reddish auburn hair color. Being introduced, with the help of Dick to designer labels she never wore, she reinvented herself into a fashion maven. During their scandalous affair, he was very generous and she had money to shop at boutiques she never could have envisioned.

Prior to his misfortune, he had given her money to augment her breast from a 34A to a 34C by one of his best friends that was a plastic surgeon that also worked miracles on Amanda after she had Ryan. Working out more at the gym became her routine and the icing on the cake was the eye candy she couldn't ignore,

Landon. She was determined to make him succumb to her and wasn't going to give up that easily. As Landon sped off, she jumped into her car and began to follow him. She couldn't fathom why Landon wouldn't give her the time of day. In her mind, she was stunning. She followed Landon to his first errand, and it wasn't your typical errand run like your dry cleaners, the bank, or the store. This errand was a nice house in a nice neighborhood with a beautiful black Porsche parked in the driveway. She had seen this car before the night she was at the restaurant where Landon was dining with a female she could not make out. When the woman left in that Porsche, she followed until she got close to the police station and turned around. She sat there and watched Landon sitting in his car on the phone. Not being able to take it any longer that the errand was another woman, she took off.

Landon saw Amanda's car in the driveway, but to not be disrespectful, he decided to call her. As he worked the phone, he steadied his breathing. Damn, this woman still gave him butterflies.

"Hello," Amanda said seeing Landon's name flash on her cellphone.

"Hey Babe, I typically don't have stalker tendencies, but I need to see you. I'm parked outside and was wondering if I could come in?" Landon pleaded.

She couldn't believe what he just told her as she looked out of her window and saw his car. Thank goodness Stevie had just left. That was too close for comfort. Not knowing how to respond and not wanting to start an argument she gave in with a soft, "Sure, come in."

Landon could not get to the door fast enough and Amanda had the door open waiting for his entrance. As he walked in, he leaned over and kissed Amanda on the cheek. Attempting to make small talk, he said, "Your place is coming together nicely."

"Yeah, I have some small items I would like to incorporate to put it all together, but Ryan and I are happy here," she said trying to continue a fluid flow with no confrontational innuendos.

"As usual, you look amazing," Landon complimented.

"Thank you, Landon. You want anything to drink?" Amanda questioned still keeping the conversation light.

"No, thank you," he said grabbing her hand and pulling her closer to him.

Even though conflicted and confused with both Stevie and Landon, Amanda could not resist his embrace. They held one another with nothing being said.

"Playing someone…the concept of pulling strings at all times, without the other party knowing, or even suspecting anything. Why do we do it? Because we can.

— GINA WINGS

Lenny could not wait to redeem himself and show Dick he was worthy of his presence. Flying down the Dallas Tollway he saw flashing lights behind him. Nervous as shit, he was prepared to get a ticket. To his surprise, the patrol car whizzed passed him in a flash and he dodged that bullet. He finally reached Dick's place. Wiping sweat from his brow all the while he was trying to maintain his cool, he knocked on Dick's door.

"Hey man, you look good walking up to this door," Lenny said still in disbelief he was walking.

"Well you have pep in your step. What's up?" Dick said noticing a different attitude from Lenny.

"Man I am happy you are on your feet, but you might want to sit down for this one," he said finally feeling he brought some value and some answers to Dick's plan.

"Well don't make me wait too long. What the hell did you find out?" Dick said smiling.

"First things first. Your girl, Taylor, well she is infatuated by the trainer Landon. She followed him to a home and I used my phone to research who occupied that lovely place. You won't believe who lives in that house!"

"Ok Lenny, enough of the theatrics. Who the hell lives there?" Dick said slightly perturbed.

"Doc, I hit the jackpot. It's your ex, Amanda!" Lenny said wanting to laugh, but withheld his disrespect to Dick.

Dick's eyes rose to a level that would heighten anyone's blood pressure to a stroke. He could not believe what he was hearing.

"Amanda? Dick said questioning what he was just told. He started to rub his brow and then his leg trying to understand why both exes wanted this dude.

"Looks like they have been an item for a minute man," Lenny said happy he offered information that had redeemed himself.

"Well this is going to be short lived for her," Dick said contemplating his next move.

"Man I thought you wanted Taylor back. What the hell do you care about Amanda, except for that bitch coughing up the money she took?" Lenny said like a gangster.

"Lenny, you are right. Good for her she found someone that wants her lame ass. I just want my money," he said ready to meet head on with Amanda.

Dick was obviously pissed, but enjoyed that fact he could walk across the floor back and forth as he tried to decide his next move. He took for granted the simple easy things in life, like waking up each morning, walking, talking, etc. It is a different story now and a huge achievement. Dick continued to pace creating too many ideas building in his head.

He blurted out, "Lenny, keep following Taylor and when I am ready, I want you to arrange for our lustful eyes to meet coincidentally being in the same place so I can enjoy the surprise on her face when she sees me walking. That shit is going to be priceless."

Continuing to take great pride in his ability to pace the floor, he blurted out "Keep close tabs on Amanda as well. It's time to get what's mine."

"No problem doc, just tell me when and I will arrange it," Lenny said like he was the first officer of a new mission.

* * *

Amanda could not believe what Stevie just told her. Dick was walking, and with that she knew she was in trouble. Beating him at his own game meant she needed to elevate hers. Trouble was surrounding her. Landon wasn't ready to let go of her to be with his crazy ex, and she had strong feelings for Stevie she should not have. After the infidelity games that were played on her, they were definitely not in her repertoire. She did not want to inflict pain on those she cared about, which was the exact opposite that was cast on her. Confusion consumed her mind. Her inner turmoil was suddenly interrupted by a call from Jessica.

"Hey Jess," Amanda said coyly afraid to divulge information Stevie got from his guy casing David.

"Well, I tried to get some answers from David without him catching on that I was on to his ass," she sheepishly said.

"Jess, I know you couldn't help it, but I don't want you to mess this shit up. Please don't!" Amanda pleaded.

"I know. I just thought if I asked some questions he might slip up," she said trying to convince Amanda to not be too concerned.

"Love you girl, but that's where you lack knowledge. These sneaky motherfuckers are not going to give you a free pass to hang them and that is why I have Stevie's guys on the case okay. Please promise me you will stop before you compromise you and your sons' well-being," Amanda said delivering the order.

"Okay Amanda but I am getting tired and I want this shit over with!" Jessica yelled.

Amanda paused for a while debating to tell Jessica what had been discovered about David. She felt a vibe that said not yet, because Jessica had demonstrated not taking instructions very well.

"I know sis please be patient, with Stevie's resources you are in good hands. His crew is very proficient with getting him what he needs, and if he has to fly there to get David in check he will. So please be patient," she said trying to keep Jessica on track.

Finishing the conversation with Jessica about David's whereabouts and not letting on all that she knew, Amanda's thoughts reverted to Stevie's news that Dick was on the move again without a handicap.

"Well I don't want you to worry, but I want to update you on a complex situation," Amanda stated not knowing if she should share this information right now with Jessica's current disposition. Then again, sharing the information could distract Jessica from her own situation.

"I know what it is, your conflicting affection for Landon," she said sounding like a smartass.

"No, this is pretty serious. Are you ready?" Amanda said about to spill the beans.

"I'm sitting down for this one," Jessica said with great anticipation.

"Stevie had been doing his surveillance to see what the hell Dick had been up to and….." She hesitated trying not to cry and then released the beast, "He camped out on a whim outside of Dick's office and saw him getting out of the driver side of a Range Rover and proceeded to walk to the office door."

There was total silence to Amanda's surprise and she said, "Jess are you still there?"

"Amanda, I am speechless. That asshole is walking?" she said in total shock.

"Yes, and now I am scared more than ever, but I trust Stevie with my life. He handled it the last time and he will handle it again," she said trying to convince her.

"Amanda put me on the backburner. You sharing this with me has me scared. I think I know what lengths your crazy ex will go to, but he may be so angry that he may harm you this time," Jessica said worried.

"I know Jess, but we are not going to divert from our initial plan. I trust Stevie with my life and yours. Listen to me; stay off of David's radar and I will be in touch soon."

"Love you Amanda. Please be careful," Jessica pleaded with her most valued friend as they hung up. Her worry for her friend overcame the issues she could barely handle before this call. Before she could stand up again, she sent a plea upwards for her friend's safety.

You Can Run, but You Can't Hide

*You can try to escape from your real or
imagined fears-but they'll catch up
with you eventually*

— THE FREE DICTIONARY.COM

David's time was running out and he knew it. It was time to come clean to some extent, but he had to test the waters to see how much Jessica knew. Depending on how much she did or did not know would determine his next step to keep his façade ongoing. He arrived home slightly earlier than the usual time after a hard day at work. The kitchen aroma smelled of fresh garlic and herbs. David knew that smell meant Jess was probably making meatloaf and garlic mash potatoes. As he walked in the kitchen, he startled Jessica because her mind was still running Amanda's news and all the many possibilities of consequences through short reels. Each scenario played worse than the last causing her heart to race and distract her from the task at hand.

"Shit, David! You scared me. Why didn't you call me and tell me when you were coming home?"

He threw out a big ass lie, "After your call the other day about picking the boys up, I thought I would surprise you and the boys since I realized it had been awhile since all of us ate together and spent time together like we used to."

Jessica did her best not to display her theatrics and thoughts that the bastard was lame and lying. She smiled in what she hoped was an admiring way and responded, "Glad you are here. I will get the table set and we can all eat as a family."

The boys ran downstairs at their dad's summoning. They, of course, were ecstatic to see their dad and scarfed down their dinner. Or at their age maybe they were just ecstatic that there was food in front of their faces. It was hard for her to tell these days. David even went so far as to rent a movie off of the cable. Did he forget he didn't pay the bill and it was cut off at one time? But low and behold it was back on. Jessica pushed her nails into her palms to remind herself to go along with that bullshit as long as she could. She let him enjoy the boys, but she had a hard time sitting still and used every excuse she could not to be in the same room as him. Her actions went unnoticed she was sure because the men were entranced by the action film. When it was time for David to face the music to come upstairs and go to bed, Jess couldn't help herself anymore. She knew what Amanda told her to do or really not to do, but she was not going to sleep with that bastard sleeping in the same bed as her with his lies. Then again, he appeared to be nice tonight and attempted to spend quality time with the family. If she acted too mad at him and he noticed, what would she say she was mad about? That he came home early and bonded with them. Jess was beyond frustrated. What to do? What to do?

*　　*　　*

Amanda was still nervous about Dick's miracle and had to call Stevie. Stevie saw it was Amanda and picked up on the first ring.

"Hey beautiful is everything alright?"

He knew there was no way anything was right with her at the moment. Not after the bombshell he dropped on her. Of course, with Amanda, something else could have happened since he last saw her.

"No," she said abruptly, but in a soft tone that portrayed that he wasn't her problem.

"Is something going on in the house, because I'm on my way," he said ready to do battle.

"No everything is okay…so far so good, but I don't know how long that is going to last," she said worried.

"You know I'm going to handle whatever comes your way. Speaking of which, I thought it would be a good idea for me to hideaway whatever money you have left in the safe and to know the banks you made the deposits to. I'm thinking I should hold on to it again for you since Dick is on the move and we don't want him to gain access to it from any route. Neko can keep an eye on it."

He offered the ballsy move as something to help make her feel safe and like she was doing something to guard herself from her ex.

Amanda was a little hesitant to respond, as she knew Stevie would be furious with what she had to say. She softly responded, "I was uncomfortable trying to move that money to all those different banks in Dallas so I just kept it in the safe."

"What!" Stevie screamed.

He couldn't believe what just came out of her mouth. After a calming breath, he asked, "How much is in there if I can ask?"

"Not that much about $375,000. After you took care of your guys from Detroit, I gave you and Neko a well-deserved payout, bought my home, and gave Jessica money so she could get her bills caught up and wouldn't lose her house, that is what is left," she said defending her decision.

"Baby, I am sorry I screamed at you, but money is money and I wanted you to secure it. As I said before, I would feel better if I stayed there. I am on my way," he said in lightening fashion. The rest of this conversation was going to be in person with him on guard.

Before she could respond to not come over just yet, Stevie had hung up. She didn't want to call him back, because when he has his mind set, there is no changing it. Plus, part of her wanted him here with her. Fear consumed her body in a way she never felt. Pain began to shoot in her legs and back from nowhere. Feeling the discomfort did not stop her from doing what she felt she needed to do. She went to her closet and pulled out her big Louis Vuitton duffle bag and proceeded to her safe that was disguised to be a small dresser in the corner of her closet. She transferred what was in the safe to the bag and climbed on her ladder to place on top shelf with her other luggage and handbags. She knew that probably wasn't the safest place or smartest thing to do. But if someone were coming to look for the money, the safe was the first place they would look. Her pains began to subside, but she still was a nervous wreck. She knew she would feel protected once Stevie got to the house. Once the money was in his care, maybe she would feel a little bit better that it was further from Dick's grasp.

*   *   *

Jessica played it safe and decided not to act out against David when he came upstairs to go to sleep. Painful has it had been to sleep next to the bastard; she did exactly what Amanda said. The next morning, she woke up at her normal time and made breakfast for the family. David decided to hang out at the house. She was so pissed he had the audacity to try to act like a present husband and father. She was so angry she found an excuse to leave the house herself.

She told him, "I need to go to the store, but I won't be gone long."

"Okay, I'm just hanging out with the boys," he said playing Dad. He was glad Jessica had left so he could call Julie with some demands.

"Hey sister-in-law," David yelled.

"What do you want David?" Julie said ready to rip him another one.

"Why don't we let all of this go away?" he said trying to negotiate.

"And how do you suppose we do that?" Julie said.

"You have your ways. Have our brother-in-law give you $100,000. You get $50,000 and I get $50,000 and neither one of us will kiss and tell," David said hoping that would help him with his current situation.

"David kiss my ass is what you can do," Julie screamed.

"Okay trick. I warned you and now you and William are going to have more problems than you could ever imagine," he threatened.

Jessica was glad she told David she had to go to the store so she could call Amanda. As Amanda was awaiting Stevie's arrival, her phone rang with Jess's call.

"Hey Jess what's up?" Amanda said nervously.

"You would have been proud of me, I kept my cool even after David pissed me off with his mister nice guy and perfect dad act," Jessica said wanting affirmation.

"Hey Jess, I hear a noise in the back of the house. I think I have some company. Can I call you back?"

Normally, Jess would have been fine with a call back, but as soon as Amanda said the words chills ran down her body. Instead, of hanging up, she just had to ask, "You are expecting someone?"

"Well Stevie is on his way, but I just got off the phone with him. He could not have made it here so quickly. Let me call you back," Amanda sounded calm and unaltered.

"Okay," Jessica replied thinking Stevie must have been closer than Amanda thought.

Amanda left her bedroom and tried to follow the noise she thought she heard. Stevie did surprise her the last time coming through the back gate, but why would he just not ring the doorbell since he had already notified her of his impending arrival. As she entered the kitchen, she suddenly felt something around her neck and a cloth over her nose. Whatever was around her neck tightened painfully closing her airway before she could even start to fight. Her sharp breaths in weren't rewarding and instead it became dark. A flash of her body struggling and glass shattering ran through her consciousness before blacking out completely.

When Amanda came to, she was disoriented and had a feeling some time had passed. She had a pain in her neck and her hands were tied behind her. Amanda breathed deeply assessing her body and trying to get a feel of her environment. Adrenaline started pumping through her veins as her system went on high alert. She could feel she was seated in a cold aluminum chair. Her mind couldn't believe what just happened and was slow to process. As the fog cleared and she realized she didn't think she had any major injuries – or any that she could feel - she tried to figure out who put her in this position. At the exact moment she thought the question, a woman's voice teased her and frankly, scared her half to death.

"You ruined my future with my future husband, twice!"

"What are you talking about and who are you?" Amanda cried. Her mouth could work, but her eyes were blindfolded.

"It's too early for you to know who I am," the voice replied from a short distance.

As Amanda wept as quietly as she could, she could hear some voices of men faintly in the background. As the voices got closer, she heard, "Hi honey." The man's smooth voice said and she could hear what she thought was an exchange of affection. She knew that voice and was mortified. She silently started to pray and yearning to telepathically send her location to Stevie for him to somehow find her.

*   *   *

Stevie got to Amanda's and no one answered when he knocked on the front door. "Damn, that woman!" Stevie muttered. She knew he was on his way over and yet he liked that she always made him work for her company. He again went to the back thinking she was at the pool and remembering the view of her in her bathing suit. There was no sign of her in any of the lounge chairs. This time he knew something was amiss. He walked to the back door of the kitchen and the door was open. He could tell there was a struggle with broken glass on the floor that was not cleaned up and spatters of red dots. He was hyperventilating and could barely breathe. He knew someone got to Amanda and it had to be Dick.

Stevie overcame his fear enough to switch into hunting mode. He swiftly went through each room of the house noting any evidence of where she might be and hoping to God he didn't find her body. When he went into Amanda's bedroom, it was ransacked. Her closet was destroyed and what look like where a piece of large furniture lived was gone. All he could think about was it had to be the safe. He knew he told her to take the money out, but wasn't sure if she did or was waiting on him. He had his hunches about Amanda and knew she was smart. He wasn't going to concede so easily as to think everything of value to her was in the safe. There wasn't a single item undisturbed in the closet. As a man who's well versed in hiding places, he started to go through some of the designer rubbish, opening each up as a thief in a hurry wouldn't take the time to do – then again a random thief would have taken most of these items along with him to pawn. Shoes and bags were in disarray from the top shelf to the bottom. He started to comb through every piece of her collection and tripped over a big Louis Vuitton duffle that damn near broke his foot. He picked up the heavy bag thinking she had clothes, shoes, and god knows what in there. He opened the bag and there it was. Now, he had to find out who had her and where, because they have an empty safe and were going to be extremely pissed when they found out.

With the money in hand, Stevie left the house positive she was no longer in it. He dialed Neko who picked up after the first ring. "It's time to sniff and snuff out that rat."

Held Hostage

*: one that is involuntarily
controlled by an outside influence*

— Merriam-Webster.com

Hysterical, nervous, and losing her mind without thinking how her underhanded actions could affect her sister, Debra, Julie called William. He saw her contact name and answered, "Hey Jules you okay?"

"No damn it! I am not. David is probably going to tell my sister Jessica about us and she, in a whirlwind affect will tell our sister Debra," she said pissed after her volatile verbal exchange with David.

"Calm down, calm down David isn't that stupid. He needs an alibi and your help," William said over confident, as Dick Casey would be if he were to respond to this same situation.

"If this dumbass wants to out you, he is also doing it to himself. If he does, let me handle it and stop being so damn worried about this or you will ruin it for me to handle."

She screamed, "So now I am being held hostage by David and now you. Fuck you William! Do what you want. I can't believe I let a piece of dick get between me, my family, and my selfish ways."

"Oh, so now you have a conscience. Suit yourself Julie. Your pussy isn't that tight. I have Ericka anyway," he said as he hung up the phone.

Julie crying out of control, her tears like a monsoon wreaking havoc down her face. She knew he was a player and she wasn't the only one. She just liked what she could get from him. He'd given her enough to put a down payment for her house and to go on shopping sprees. That last exchange of words hurt to the core. She didn't mean to have feelings for him, but she couldn't help it after all the intimate time they spent together. She knew what she was doing was savage, but she wasn't that close to her sisters anyway and no one paid that much attention to Williams's activities except for his money and what he got them. So she had no conscience when it came to having an affair with William because no one else seemed to know or tune into his deceitful ways. Now she wondered if it was going to be worth the aftermath that surely was to follow.

*   *   *

Jessica was exhausted from the continuing saga of David's lies and she had not heard back from Amanda, which fed her already high level of anxiety. She decided to take matters into her own hands. Jessica made sure the boys were at Debra's house in order to keep them from the tornado that was brewing. Once she released it from her body, there was no telling the destruction that may lay in her wake. She had every intention of destroying David because his lies had already demolished the life they had built together. She knew she had to wing it to call David's bluff without having all the solid information from Stevie's guy. Shameless with his actions, David walked into the kitchen as if there was nothing he had to explain. Jessica was about to change that.

"Hey Jess, what did you cook for dinner?" David said leaning into the refrigerator looking for something to munch on.

"The question I have for you David is what have you been cooking up lately?" she said with a hiss and an eyebrow cocked.

"Cooking up? I don't know what in the world you are talking about?" he said with a smirk on his face.

That smirk infuriated Jessica, so she proceeded to bait the unsuspecting Barracuda.

"David I'm tired of you playing dumb."

For a moment, there was silence. Silence was golden, the anticipation of who was going to draw first blood… Sizing each other up once more at the game being played David felt his confession about to surface and take an ugly turn. Jessica began to click her nails on the granite island and with that nervous jester, David knew what was about to raise its ugly head.

"So you played me and our sons and took us hostage." she said with her fist balling up.

"Woman, I still don't know what in the hell you are talking about," he said pretending to be slightly confused, but his body language gave him away.

"Honey you look pinked and a bit puzzled," she said with a sinister giggle, like a tiger that had pounced on its prey and the prey was futilely attempting to fight for its freedom.

"Now who is playing games Jess?" David raised his voice hoping to feign dominance of the situation.

Jessica decided to join the shouting match and with all of her pinned up anger she screamed, "You don't have a JOB David!"

*   *   *

The aluminum chair was rock solid, hard, and cold. Most of her body was numb, stiff, and sore from the extended time without standing. When she thought no one was in her immediate vicinity, Amanda attempted to tear her duck taped hands free. Otherwise, Amanda was still, having decided to conserve her energy when it was really needed. A familiar scent of cologne reached her nose and Amanda knew a certain someone was approaching her. Her body readied itself for an insult. Stevie was right that asshole was walking. She felt the tip of an object slowly caressing her neck. She was petrified and held her breath not to be injured by the unknown sharp object.

"Well, Well, Well, Amanda we meet again, but not at our usual spot, the courtroom nor with that cowboy of a lawyer you hid behind. This venue is much more interesting my dear," Dick said continuing to rub Amanda's neck with a scalpel and ready to get down to business.

Amanda replied with a disgusted tone, "What is it you want from me?"

"Do I need to help you answer that question dear? You know what I want," he replied a little firmer.

"No, I don't Dick," Amanda screamed.

"Oh, that's right. Sometimes I forget how stupid you are," he punctuated his comment with breathing the words close to her face and jabbing the end of the scalpel into the under portion of her jaw enjoying the wince it produced from her lips. He jerked away the metal and paced in front of her. Once recomposed, he offered, "I'll give you a clue…" He paused and she could feel his body heat get closer to hers. "It has nothing to do with any disgusting piece of you."

His whisper in her ears sent chills down her body, which the over confident doctor took in the opposite meaning of them.

"See I still have that effect on you, though."

He caressed his hand down her arm to absorb the goose bumps.

Amanda jerked her arm away as far and fast as she could in her constrained position.

"I want nothing to do with any disgusting piece of you either. You may be walking, but I bet other parts of you are still as lame as ever!"

She spat the insult in what she hoped was his direction.

Dick was fuming and pacing across the floor. He was losing his composure with her annoying behavior getting under his skin. He shouted, "Look bitch I want my money!" At the same time, he snatched off her blindfold. Her eyes met his and there was nothing there but diabolical furor passing between them.

Amanda counterpunched with her response, "If I liked being called 'bitch' to my face, manipulated with lies, and disrespected with your wandering eyes, we would still be married, or better yet, you would have your money. Like I said; I don't have it! Maybe you should ask one of your other so called bitches."

With the blindfold off, Dick put the scalpel right in front of Amanda's eyes. "I know it was you, Amanda! Besides…" he played with the scalpel a bit across her smooth face…"my other bitches were much more cooperative and they all still love me and what I do to them."

Amanda held still despite her strong desire to vomit at the site of his and the gestures he made. Before she could counter, Dick slipped the blindfold back in place and her fear of where the scalpel would make contact next made the words slide back down her throat. Dick smiled at her silence and decided he'd had enough of an effect on her for now, plus he did not want to expose his surprise too early. He left her frozen there in the chair. Amanda felt his heat leave her vicinity and after a few seconds of hesitation she breathed a sigh of relief. She had survived, for now.

Masquerade

"And, after all, what is a lie?
Tis but the truth in a masquerade."

— ALEXANDER POPE

David was shocked that Jessica finally discovered his secret. He thought she was oblivious to his deception and would never catch on. Perplexed and frustrated that his lies had been brought to light, his mind raced for a believable response. Did he continue to deny it and see if he could con her once again? Or did he come clean and swallow his pride? He'd been successful for so long that he found it hard to believe she had discovered the truth on her own. David suddenly knew she had to have help and that person had to be her best friend and confidant, Amanda. With this revelation, he knew how to respond to her outburst.

"Congratulations," David said clapping his hands giving her a slow, taunting standing ovation.

"My question to you is why?" she said not impressed with his reaction.

"What do you mean why?" he wasn't about to lead her to any specific conclusion, yet.

"Why couldn't you tell me you lost your job so we could figure out a way to pay our bills and provide for the boys?"

"Damn it Jess! I was embarrassed and quite frankly, you made it difficult to continue this fantasy of a marriage," he said with some relief. There some of the truth was on the table.

"So our marriage is a fantasy. What the fuck are you trying to say?" she spat in anger as she moved closer wanting to smack him in his face. As her anger continued to build to a boiling point, Jessica said, "Is that why you had to use my sister, Julie, to console you because you failed has a husband and father?"

That comment derailed David from his initial route to deceive her once again. He wondered how in the hell did she factor Julie in this equation? Again, his thoughts went back to the only way she couldn't have known any of this… this had to have Amanda's hands in it. As his head was continuing to fill with various confusions and trying to figure out escaping this mess, he was torn on whether to expose Julie and William or to pretend to try to patch things up with Jessica until he figured out his next move. He lashed back hoping to buy a little more time to think and to get more information from her about what all she knew.

"What does Julie have to do with any of this Jess?" he said a little nervously.

"So you don't know where I am headed with this Einstein?" she said sarcastically not wanting to give up anything else she knew.

Not knowing where else to go with this conversation, he coward and said, "Think what you want." He figured she'd back down and that his blackmail attempt on Julie would work.

"Think what I want? OK, well. You can think about what I want after you are served with divorce papers, you pathetic excuse of a husband and father!" she threatened.

David staggered back pretending to be hurt by the threat, but in reality he saw the chance to exit, feigning insult and hurt. He dropped his head and wiped at his eyes as he left the house.

As soon as the door closed, Jessica let out a frustrated scream. She wasn't sure if she gained any ground or if he won that round yet again.

* * *

Dick was in Amanda's presence again, enjoying taunting Amanda's neck. He had to get out of her the answer he sought. His sociopathic mind reflected on the concept, "An eye for an eye and a tooth for a tooth."

Dick preached, "Amanda are you familiar with Exodus 21:23-25? I'm sure you're not, so let me give you the short version. The two verses in Exodus tell us the principle of how the punishment must fit the crime and there should be a penalty for evil actions."

"So now you are quoting Bible verses to validate your pathetic actions? What's the penalty for all the horrendous things you've done me and your son?" she responded angrily at the audacity he had to feel validated in his actions by using the Bible.

In his mind, that was the interpretation, even though further interpretation of the Bible of "An eye for an eye" was never to be used to justify settling personal grievances. Dick completely ignored the comment and asked instead, "What's the code to the safe?" Dick had a hold of Amanda's hair and had yanked her neck backwards into an uncomfortable position.

Amanda could barely breathe in the room and could feel more eyes on her than Dick's. Did the eyes belong to his old lackeys, new ones, or the female voice she heard before? From his questioning, she figured they took the safe, but hadn't figured out that it was empty. Her brain was working overtime to find a way to survive this. Instead of answering his question, she choked out one of her own. "Who's the bitch?"

"None of your business," he spat back and yanked harder on her hair.

"Well it's lovely to meet you, Taylor."

She coughed out her guess. This made Dick let go of her hair and she gulped several deep breaths putting her head into a more natural position. Her hands pulled instinctively to rub and comfort the pain, which only brought more jolts of pain.

"Nice try. You want to try again?" said the woman's voice.

"Enough of the pleasantries; what is the code to the safe?" he said as if that was the last time he was going to ask.

Afraid of what might happen to her when he saw the money was not there and yet hoping they'd let her go when they realized she did not possess what they desired, she decided to be brave and face her fate by saying, "It's 7040."

Unbeknownst to the blindfolded Amanda, Dick motioned to the woman to enter the code. She followed his instructions as he said to Amanda, "That's an interesting choice for your safe code."

"It's Ryan's birth date and birth month backwards," she said in disgust.

Quickly unlocking and opening the safe, the woman yelled, "There's nothing in here; it's empty!"

*   *   *

Neko met Stevie at their usual meeting spot in Dallas in the back corner, minus Amanda, which had Stevie visibly upset.

"Man I came as fast as I could," Neko said as soon as he was within earshot of Stevie. The two shook hands like brothers do.

"So you know for a fact her ex is behind her sudden disappearance?" Neko asked with a concerned tone. Whoever took her had no idea the wrath they had unleashed, poor soul.

"He has to be. The safe she hid the money is gone and so is she. No one else had a motive to come for her but him, man, but when they find out there isn't any money in the safe I don't know what that crazy doc will do," Stevie explained. He stared at his drink as if it might have a solution for him.

"What do you mean the money isn't in the safe?" Neko asked after the waitress placed his glass of Hennessy on the table as if she'd perfectly timed her delivery with his arrival and he took a sip.

"When I spoke to her about the money she said she put it all in the safe and didn't put it in various banks here, like we told her. I got pretty angry and told her to get the money out of the safe and ready for me to pick up. I was going to ask you to hold it until the situation improved. Apparently, she acted quickly and put it in her Louis getaway bag. I found the overlooked bag in her ransacked closet. They took her and what they thought was a safe full of dough," Stevie spoke intensely and banged his fist on the tabletop.

"Man you got your heart invested in her. Let me and the dudes I have here track that sucker down. Trust me, we will find her," Neko offered with confidence and a hand on his friend's shoulder.

"I know you will. Start by going back to her crib. I'm sure whoever took her will go back there to case the place again looking for her stash once they crack open that safe," Stevie said as his mind was racing.

"Bet." Neko said taking the last sip of his drink and disappearing in the smoke filled club. This wasn't his first rodeo and he knew what to do.

The Fixer

A person who makes arrangements for other people, especially of an illicit or devious kind.

— Dictionary.com

Lenny's stock had risen threefold. Luck fell into his lap with his new female accomplice. This new acquisition was better than having Vernon on board and lecherous Lenny enjoyed the new eye candy. During one of Lenny's surveillance attempts to follow Taylor one evening, a new piece to the puzzle presented itself, a mystery woman. He went above and beyond to find out who she was and busted her one evening taking pictures in front of Amanda's house. Upon further investigation, he found out this woman had a history with Landon. He was very confused why two women were so interested in Amanda and stalking her residence. To his surprise, the common denominator for these women was Landon. Gloating and anxious to share this new information with Dick, Lenny came up with a plan that Dick shockingly approved of. Given the greenlight to proceed he added a new team member, Nikki, and that was the redemption Lenny needed. He was in the driver's seat again, and Nikki was more than happy to oblige with the payout he promised. Lenny thought it almost too easy to deliver to her what she wanted in the end, Landon.

*   *   *

Landon had not heard a peep from Amanda and wasn't in the mood to call her. He really wanted to get through his class and go by to see where he stood with her for better or worse. Landon just needed to know his path forward. As he tried to quickly escape the gym, Taylor was also eager to leave as well. She waved goodbye to Landon, which he was thankful she didn't pester him again, and high tailed faster than lightening to her destination. Once she arrived, she ran like a mad woman to the door and knocked. Her heart raced with anticipation not knowing what she was going to say, but no one answered. She knocked one more time and as she leaned into the door to put her ear to it to listen for movement, her weight opened it slightly. Fear filled inside her not knowing what to expect. She had built herself up to this moment and her fight or flight senses were sending conflicting messages. Curiosity, however, won out and made her to continue to walk inside. As she entered the threshold and surveyed the scene before her, she wondered why this other woman had the upper hand when it came to Landon. Her taste was obviously less delectable than hers. As she made her way through the house, she could see something bad had happened. Unwilling to put herself in any more danger, Taylor turned to leave, but a hand touched her neck and she screamed in disbelief.

"What in the hell are you doing here?" Landon yelled, keeping a firm grip on her.

"Oh Shit! You scared me," Taylor said breathlessly.

She put her hand on the one he held to her. The touch calmed her and brought forth another reason for her heart to flutter.

Before the two of them could say another word or move another inch, they both found themselves looking down the barrel of a gun. Landon instinctively pushed Taylor behind him and put his hands up in the air. The culprits had returned. Landon looked as if he had seen a ghost and Lenny looked as if he had hit another Jackpot. Landon and Nikki's eyes met with unfinished business and Lenny and Taylor's eyes met with the bad blood between them from the failures of their prior meeting.

"Don't move!" Lenny spoke forcefully.

Taylor's pale face was filled with fear, as she knew exactly what Lenny was capable of. She did exactly what Lenny commanded and stayed in her spot right behind Landon.

"Hey baby," Nikki said as she looked into Landon's sterile eyes.

Lenny had given Nikki her directives beforehand as well as a weapon. She was more than happy to keep Landon in an unfamiliar predicament. For the first time in a long time, she had Landon's full attention and the upper hand.

Landon with his hands still in the air asked, "Where is Amanda?"

Nikki smiled with contempt and answered, "Right where she belongs." She motioned with her gun for Landon to take a seat. She handed her gun to Lenny, who pointed one at each victim. Nikki then proceeded to tie Landon to the chair. Fortunately, she'd done this before and wasted no time securing him and then retrieving her gun again.

With Landon out of the way, Lenny took Taylor out of the house by her hair and instructed Nikki, "Stay here and you better not move."

Nikki never took her eyes off Landon as she happily replied, "I'm not going anywhere because what I want is right here."

She looked lustfully down at Landon tied to the chair. "I will be waiting on your call Lenny."

As Lenny escorted Taylor to his car to get back to Dick, Neko was at a distance watching the circus perform. Lenny was so excited that he had found Dick's prize possession that he got sloppy and was unaware that he was being tailed. Neko could have interrupted the show, but none of the characters were the one he sought. They were mere busy bees he could follow back to sweet honey.

*   *   *

Dick enjoyed taunting Amanda, but was tired of waiting for Lenny to finish what they had started. Always prepared, he decided to add fuel to the fire.

He opened a cooler containing all types of beverages, including wine and beer, but carefully selected a bottle of water. He emptied some of the water and added something else to it and vigorously shook its contents. As he approached Amanda with her blindfold still intact, he instructed, "I am sure you are thirsty by now and need something to drink," Dick placed the bottle right up to her lips.

"No, thank you," she curtly responded through clenched teeth. She knew better than to accept any kindness from this man.

Without negotiating, he pulled her hair yanking her head back making her yelp. Once her mouth opened, he drowned her with the water, making sure she drank enough for the drug to have an effect. Gagging attempting not to drink and putting up a furious fight; she lost the battle as hard as she fought, and he got the job done. As Amanda sat in her chair with water drooling from her mouth, Dick took her blindfold off and enjoyed watching the show. Amanda's face had fear written all over it. Her eyes scanned the room, but she couldn't quite see. Amanda began to have an out of body experience. Her body was aware of the room and she felt herself tied to the chair, but was not able to move. Amanda saw herself outside of her body as a mummy not able to speak or move.

"You feel alright Amanda? You look a bit peeked," he said laughing.

She could make out his shape and hear his gregarious hateful tone, but could not react. Amanda couldn't feel her mouth even though she thought she was moving her lips with a snide remark. She couldn't formulate a sound. Her ability not to react with her impaired motor function confirmed Dick's administering Ketamine was taking its affect. Amanda was succumbing to a drug she could not control.

The Closer

A person who is skilled at bringing a business transaction to a satisfactory conclusion.

DICTIONARY.COM

Neko dialed Stevie and informed him about what had transpired. "Man this shit is crazy," Neko relayed to Stevie.

"What's going on Neko?" Stevie said concerned. He was ready for some good news as he hadn't made any progress with is efforts.

"Shortly after I got to Amanda's, Lenny turned up with a female accomplice. They walked right on in as if the door was already open and they had every right to be there. I started to get a closer look, but then this fool left the house with a skinny ass pseudo red head chick I guess that was already there. I sent a tail with them while I stayed here to see what the other female was up to. And you know what fool was in the house with her? That punk ass Amanda was hanging with. He's all tied up and she's got a piece pointed at him," he blurted all he'd seen in one breath.

Stevie was filled with fury after hearing that not only was Lenny involved, which was bad news in itself, but that Landon and a red head were in attendance. The red head could only be one person tied to all the rest, Taylor. "Good call, Neko. That red head is likely Dick's ex, Taylor. The question is why was she there and why'd she leave with Lenny?"

"It didn't look like she was a willing participant, if that helps," Neko added.

"Maybe. My gut says Lenny was taking her back to Dick and we know Dick has Amanda. Neko, can you catch up to your guys?"

Stevie felt like they were getting closer to finding her, which grew his desire to hurt a certain someone since the other someone was tied up at the moment – literally.

"I certainly can and I got an idea for what to do when we get there." Neko felt a battle coming and he was ready.

"You know how I did a Houdini in the courtroom? I think that is how we can play this shit that's about to go down!"

"Use your best judgement, Neko. I trust you to do this because at this point someone is going to die at my hands and at this time I am the wrong person to end this saga. Whatever you need to do, do it!" Stevie said not hesitating confirmation of the order.

Neko hung up and did not waste any time putting the plan in action as he did before. He got his new soldiers in place with their directives as they were tailing Lenny. Neko's guys were in route and ready for action.

Neko wasn't far behind as he tracked their location with his phone.

By the time Lenny pulled into a parking space in a mostly empty lot, which belonged to a warehouse suite in the Dallas Industrial District, Lenny had already informed Dick he was on his way back while Nikki was commanding the post and looking for the money at Amanda's. Dick was happy to hear they had also captured new leverage to use against Amanda in the form of her beau, Landon. Once Lenny and his new companion, Taylor, emerged from his vehicle, Lenny took a firm hold on Taylor with one hand while still holding his gun with the other. When Taylor entered the warehouse, the first thing her eyes fixated on was the sight of the back of a woman clearly restrained in a chair. She froze and tried going back out the door. As the Lenny jumped to keep her from running out the door, Dick entered the open space sounding like the voice of Oz, "And here enters my lost love."

Lenny would have laughed if he weren't struggling to keep the lost love in place. Taylor froze in her spot. Her tear-filled eyes became larger than life and she hoped her ears were not playing tricks on her when she heard the familiar voice. She knew it was Dick and she really hoped his presence meant she wasn't going to join the other lady in the chair.

"Don't I get a hug?" He said smiling, ready to see her reaction to the great reveal.

Taylor turned around to the voice and watched Dick as he walked towards her. At that moment between thinking she was going to die to the shock of seeing a miracle, her brain and body could not process so much information and she fainted.

* * *

Landon looked at Nikki and asked her, "Why are you doing this?"

"Why am I doing this? I love you Landon. Don't you know that by now?" she said matter of fact.

Landon just stared back at her. He knew Nikki had mental issues and talking to her when she's like this, without a mental health professional present, was a losing situation. There wasn't anything he could formulate to say that she would remotely comprehend. To her, she wasn't processing the fact that she tied him to a chair and that he was in her presence against his will. All she saw was him in front of her and they were together, which was all that she wanted.

After a pause, she said, "Oh hey, do you know where this Amanda lady would hide $900k? I'm supposed to find it while I'm here."

Landon's jaw dropped. "Uh, no. I had no idea she had that kind of money."

He actually didn't know where the money was and he was rather shocked she hadn't said anything. Then again they were always busy doing other things than chatting about their finances.

Nikki stared at him for a long moment and then said, "OK, well, I have to find it so sit tight sweetie. I'll be back before you know it."

She kissed him on the cheek and pranced off to start her treasure hunt.

As soon as she was out of sight, Landon began working on the ties. He couldn't sit still with this woman when his main concern was for Amanda's welfare, especially after seeing whom he saw tonight and knowing close to a million dollars was on the line.

Redemption

"Redemption just means you just make a change in your life and you try to do right, versus what you were doing, which was wrong."

— Ice T

Nikki was confident Landon wasn't going anywhere, so she went to work looking for the money Lenny told her had to be there. She was told she would be handsomely rewarded if she found it, and then she could run away with her man, Landon. As she searched the house, she tried to think where she would hide that kind of money, so she headed straight for the master closet. Once in there, she was distracted by the clothes and shoes and handbags…ponding which ones she should take for their trip. Unfortunately for Nikki, with a little help from Stevie, a 911 call was placed for a possible breaking and entering. While Nikki was consumed with the name brands, she failed to notice the police arrive nor did she know they had already found and freed her man downstairs by the time they found her in the closet with her hands full of everything but her gun. Nikki immediately claimed she was the homeowner; however, this lie was revoked when she could not provide the necessary identification to the policemen. The gun in her possession and Landon tied to the chair did not help her situation either. After they had her in handcuffs and in the back of a squad car, Landon provided information to the police on how he got there and what had transpired. Nikki was going ballistic at her separation from Landon. When the police officer tried to question her at the scene, all Nikki could talk about was how Lenny had told her she would have Landon. In what would have sounded like chaotic babble had Landon not helped decipher, Nikki spilled the beans on the whole plan between finding the money and Amanda's kidnapping and Lenny promising her Landon. She kept repeating, "Lenny promised, Lenny promised..." She shared enough valid information to send squad cars full speed ahead to the warehouse for a possible kidnapping and hostage scenario. As much as Landon wished he could join the rescue, he stayed back at Amanda's and watched them take Nikki away. He would be escorted in another vehicle to the precinct to make an official statement after the medics finished giving him a quick once over.

* * *

As soon as Stevie realized what was going on at Amanda's house, he called Neko to get the crew out of sight, "Hey man Five-0 is on their way. They got the intruder in Amanda's house and she sang like a bird."

"Thanks for the heads up. My dudes here already completed the plan I put in place, so, if they are on their way, we're out of here," Neko said happy that the mission had been accomplished.

"I'm good with the crew leaving, but I need you to make sure nothing has happened to Amanda. So can you stay out of the cops' way, but close enough to report what's happening?" Stevie asked uncomfortable not knowing the unknown.

"Bet. After what the crew set up, I don't think we are going have to worry about the good doctor or his flunky," Neko said.

Stevie took some comfort in this news, but wouldn't relax until he had Amanda back in his arms.

"Thank you, Neko."

* * *

Taylor finally recovered from fainting. When she opened her eyes, she found herself seated next to Dick, who was stroking her hair and looking into her eyes still deeply in love with her and full of worry. Her heart wrenched and then she remembered what she saw. Having difficulty formulating her words Taylor said, "How, when, Dick you are walking! That is great."

She moved over to hug him and he embraced her tightly.

"Yes. Baby I'm back and I forgive you for leaving me, but I won't forget it," he said like he was scolding a child.

"I was confused, Dick, and was traumatized by everything that happened. I am sorry and have thought of you often."

She attempted to excuse her behavior.

"I'm also going to forgive you for chasing the trainer," he said letting her know he knew her every move.

She didn't have anything to say and held her head down with Dick's remark about Landon. He grabbed her chin and kissed her forehead and said, "No worries baby. You'll make it up to me."

"Of course, I will."

They sealed the promise with a kiss.

Lenny had grabbed a beer out of the cooler and was sipping it as he leaned against a wall observing Amanda's inability to communicate and the exchange between the rekindled lovebirds. He looked at Dick and said, "I'm about to call our girl to see if she found anything at the house. In the meantime, what's the plan for your ex?"

"Find out if anything is there and if so, get it to me. If she doesn't find anything, I have other ways to get it out of Amanda. At the end of the day, we are going to take care of her, and I don't care how it gets done," Dick said.

He took Taylor's hand and told Lenny, "Taylor and I have some catching up to do. I will be in contact," Dick winked at Lenny and smiled. Still holding Taylor's hand, he walked over to Amanda and said, "Checkmate Bitch!"

Amanda heard everything and wanted so badly to smack the shit out of him, but she could do nothing.

Dick opened the passenger door to his Range Rover for Taylor. She jumped in and they took off. Neko saw Dick and Taylor turn the corner to where he was posted. He also saw the cop cars speeding towards the warehouse, which the Range Rover didn't seem to notice. Inside the warehouse, Lenny dialed Nikki on his cellphone to get an update and continued sipping on his beer. He got no answer from Nikki, which made Lenny's brow crease. Maybe she had her hands full with all the money and her lame ass man. As he returned his phone to his pocket, Dallas' finest busted through the warehouse doors with guns drawn. They screamed at both bodies to put their hands up, but quickly assessed that the female wasn't a threat and therefore turned to the male in the room. Lenny was startled and attempted to follow their direction, but one hand struggled to get out of his pocket and the other dropped his bottleneck. With the bang and shatter of the glass, one officer screamed, "He's got a gun!" Bullets started to fly. Within seconds of the officers entering the room, Lenny perished to the floor along with his beer and the echoes were fading.

Before their eardrums could adapt, the warehouse shook with a loud explosion a very short distance away. Smoke filled the air above the street in close proximity to the warehouse giving away the location of the blast. Some of the officers went towards the area where the black smoke was billowing and others remained to assess the threat within the warehouse and the condition of the victim, Amanda. The man lying on the floor that was shot, Lenny, was ignored after someone approached and confirmed his fate. His body would remain in place until the coroner arrived. Sirens were heard storming towards the scene of the explosion. Neko's mission was accomplished. Now he just had to sit and wait for Amanda to come out.

Apologetically Unapologetic

: shows regretful acknowledgement of an offense or failure, but refuses to say sorry causing someone problems or unhappiness.

— DICTIONARY.COM

Amanda awoke in a hospital bed to the two nervous, but smiling faces of Stevie and Neko.

"Baby, you had us scared there for a minute," Stevie said has he kissed Amanda's forehead over and over again.

"Yeah Ma, you had us scared for real," Neko said.

All three of them laughed in unison at Neko's comment. Although Amanda's laugh was weak, she was happy she seemed to have feeling of her body again.

"You saved me again, didn't you?"

She looked at each face for confirmation. When they nodded, she thanked them.

"I don't know how to repay my guardian angels," Amanda said with a strained voice. She then proceeded to ask, "What happened? I remember some of the events that transpired, but some are really foggy to me."

Neko and Stevie looked at one another trying to determine how to answer Amanda's questions. Before they could get started, her cellphone began to ring.

"You want me to take the call, baby?" Stevie said.

"No, I got it. Hello," Amanda said softly.

"Amanda, it's Jess. How are you doing? Stevie called me to tell me, well what I started to uncover on David's ass, and also to tell me what happened to you," she said concerned.

"I'm doing okay. I am in good hands," Amanda said as she looked at Stevie.

"I have no doubt you are, but I told the owner of those hands I wouldn't believe it until I saw it, so Stevie got me a ticket to come down to see you! That handsome man also had his boys put David in check and I am not going to have any problems from him."

She boasted her win and was so ready to get to Dallas as soon as possible.

"That's what my man does," Amanda whispered as her throat grew dry.

"Amanda we will talk soon, just take care and we have a lot to talk about," Jess said talking ninety miles a minute.

"I will," Amanda responded before putting the phone down. Amanda looked at Neko and Stevie and said, "Thank you for taking care of not only me, but my best friend. That means a lot to me."

"You know I would do anything for you Amanda," Stevie said holding her hand and offering her a sip of water with the other. After she took a sip, she pulled as much as she could for him to lean in and kiss her.

"Do I need to leave this love fest?" Neko interrupted.

"No, Neko. You and Stevie are family to me and I don't know how to ever repay you," she said.

Neko looked at Stevie then Amanda and said, "I'm going to let you all figure that one out."

They laughed and then Amanda got serious and said, "What happened?"

"Babe that crazy ass ex kidnapped you, tried to find the money, had Landon's ex kidnap his ass, and he captured Taylor as well," Stevie tried to continue, but Amanda interrupted.

"Tried to kidnap Landon! Is he okay?"

"He is fine," Stevie assured her, but he was perturbed by her concern. "Without Neko on the scene, I may have not found you," he said a bit choked up. He continued, "Your ex drugged you, Lenny found the Taylor chick Dick was having the affair with and delivered her to your ex and the rest is history. Bottom line you are safe."

"What do you mean the rest is history?" Amanda saw the look the two men exchanged and the slight curve to their lips, which meant there was way more to the story than they were letting on.

"The police shot and killed Lenny after busting into the warehouse. Meanwhile, your ex and his girl drove off, but their car blew up before they could get far," Stevie said matter of fact and with a straight face as if he weren't secretly doing cartwheels in his head from the joy of the end of it all.

Amanda blinked several times as if each blink helped her process the shocking information that just came out of Stevie's mouth. The room fell silent. The pause was long enough to become uncomfortable before Amanda broke it with, "Neither one of them will ever bother me again?"

Neko and Stevie laughed and simultaneously said, "NO." This is why they liked her so much. She saw past all the details and the good outcome that came from them.

*   *   *

Jessica made her way down to Dallas and spent a few days with Amanda to ensure her recovery went well. Luckily, Amanda was back to her normal self after the drugs wore off, the care of a few phenomenal nurses, and a few good meals. Upon her release from the hospital, Jessica surprised Amanda with a trip back to Cove Island. Jessica had taken care of all the details, including Ryan's care, and pushed her friend to let go for a little bit in order to help process all the trauma. Amanda was glad for the trip and only felt a little guilty that she thought going through the drama was worth the freedom she felt now. She felt like the doctors had told her she was cancer free after years of pain and suffering.

On the plane ride to the Caribbean, in first class no less, Jessica got Amanda caught up on how Stevie and Neko's crew scared David so badly that he gave up everything that was left. This time it would be his ass that had to start over. Jessica also filled Amanda in on her scandalous sister, Julie, cheating with her other sister's husband, William. Unbeknownst to them all, Debra knew about Williams's shenanigans and had taken action to make sure she was taken care of when the day came that he would be revealed as the unsavory character he really was. Debra was a smart cookie and had stocked piled money in secret accounts, which Jessica whispered to Amanda as no one was supposed to know. Jessica assured Amanda that her sister would be fine and was all too glad to be divorcing that cheater. They chatted non-stop the entire flight. They barely paused to eat or use the facilities.

As Amanda had once done for her friend, Jessica had a car waiting for them at the airport to take them to the hotel. The pair quickly checked in and changed into their suits. They couldn't wait to lounge by the pool, soak up the sun, and drink something fruity. They made note of all they were thankful for and how things may actually start to calm down. Just as Jessica suggested a toast, a server appeared with two bubbling glasses of Champagne, which they hadn't ordered. Amanda said thank you, but didn't look at the server as she was distracted by all the information Jessica had downloaded onto her and the fact that something was off about her drink. Jessica, however, was in on the delivery and winked at the server when she thanked him. While Amanda was trying to figure out what was bright and shiny in her drink, the server stood nearby not moving as Amanda proceeded to pick out a huge rock. Jessica's eyes bulged at the sight of it, as she was not in on the secret of how big a rock was going to be in the drink, and she giggled at the sight of her friend's face. Amanda stared at what she pulled out of her drink for some time before she looked over at her dear friend. Jessica was too tickled to speak and merely pointed.

Amanda followed her finger sliding the huge diamond ring that fit perfectly. She pulled her shades off and looked at the server for the first time. It was Stevie! He came forward, kneeled next to her lounger, and caressed her hand, while magically rubbing the shiny rock. "Amanda…"

Index

1. "apologetically unapologetic". In Dictionary.com,
   Accessed April, 2018.
   http:// www.dictionary.com

2. Brown, Bobby. October 11, 1988. "My
   Prerogative",
   Bobby Brown, MCA,
   Accessed April, 2018.

3. Bushnell, Candace. (n.d.) Goodreads.com,
   Accessed November, 2017.
   http://www.goodreads.com.

4. "by any means necessary". 2018. In Merriam-
   Webster.com.
   Accessed April, 2018.
   http:// www.merriam-webster.com.

5. Campbell, Nenia. (n.d.) Bestquotes4ever.com,
   Accessed March, 2018.
   http://www.bestquotes4ever.com.

6. Cena, John. (n.d.) Inspiringquotes.us,
   Accessed March, 2018.
   http://www.inspiringquotes.us.

7. Confucious. (n.d.) Goodreads.com,
   Accessed March,k 2018.
   http://www.goodreads.com.

8. DeWalt, Jaeda. (n.d.) Goodreads.com,
   Accessed March, 2018.
   http:// www.goodreads.com

9. Dix, Dorothy. (n.d.) BrainyQuote.com,
   Accessed March, 2018.
   http://www.brainyquote.com.

10. Fifth Harmony. September 27, 2016. "That's My Girl",
    Fifth Harmony, Epic Syco,
    Accessed March, 2018.

11. Fitzpatrick, Becca. (n.d.) Azquotes.com,
    Accessed March, 2018.
    http://www.azquotes.com .

12. "held hostage". In Merriam-Webster.com.
Accessed April, 2018.
http://www.merriam-webster.com.

13. Hope, Donna Lynn. (n.d.) Goodreads.com,
Accessed April, 2018.
http://www.goodreads.com.

14. Humphrey, Humbert. (n.d.) Goodreads.com,
Accessed December, 2017.
http://www.goodreads.com.

15. Ice T. (n.d.) BrainyQuote.com,
Accessed April, 2018.
http://www.brainyquote.com.

16. Katrina and the Waves. April 26, 1985. "Walking
on Sunshine".
Katrina and the Waves, Attic-Capitol,
Accessed April, 2017.

17. Lady Gaga. (n.d.) Goodreads.com,
Accessed January, 2018.
http://www.goodreads.com.

18. McWilliams, Peter. (n.d.) BrainyQuote.com,
    Accessed January, 2018.
    http://www.brainyquote.com.

19. Meyer, Joyce. (n.d.) BrainyQuote.com,
    Accessed March, 2018.
    http://www.brainyquote.com.

20. Morgan, J.P. (n.d.) Goodreads.com,
    Accessed March, 2017.
    http://www.goodreads.com.

21. Pope, Alexander. (n.d.) BrainyQuote.com,
    Accessed April, 2018.
    http://www.brainyquote.com.

22. Racine, Jean. (n.d.) BrainyQuote.com,
    Accessed March, 2018.
    http://www.brainyquote.com.

23. Tamia. February 13, 2001. "There's a Stranger in
    My House",
    Tamia, Elektra,
    Accessed March, 2018.

24. "the closer". 2018. In Dictionary.com.
    Accessed April, 2018.
    http://www.dictionary.com.

25. "the fixer". 2018. In Dictionary.com.
    Accesssed April, 2018.
    http://www. Dictionary.com.

26. Tze, Sun. (n.d.) Famousquotefrom.com.
    Accessed January, 2018.
    http://www.famousquotefrom.com.

27. Unknown. (n.d.) Pinterest.com.
    Accessed March, 2018.
    http://pinterest.com.

28. Wings, Gina. (n.d.) Goodreads.com,
    Accessed April, 2018.
    http://www.goodreads.com.

29. "you can run, but you can't hide". 2018. In
    TheFreeDictionary.com.
    Accessed April, 2018.
    http://www.thefreedictionary.com.

About The Author

Robin Munro author of her first novel *Pure Deception* continues the saga of more lies, betrayal, and deceit with the sequel and second novel *Pure Revenge*. She has been encouraged to complete the Trilogy with a third book. Stay pure-until then.

She and her son reside in Dallas, Texas.